GROWL AND PROWL

RAYMOND

NYT AND USA TODAY BESTSELLING AUTHOR
EVE LANGLAIS

PROLOGUE

RAYMOND'S LIST OF REASONS TO STAY HOME, #9: Straight A's in school brings bruises.

It broke Nana's heart to see Raymond dragging his feet as he trudged up the driveway after the bus dropped him off. His clothes were scuffed. His glasses were crooked. His younger sister Jessie wasn't with him, having pre-arranged an afterschool playdate. His older siblings, now in middle and high school, took a different bus home, meaning it was just the two of them.

Nana took one look at his dejected posture and sat him in a chair before placing in front of him some freshly made lemonade and a cookie. She said nothing. Just waited.

Eventually he said, "I had a bad day."

"I would have never guessed." She tried to sound

light, but inside, her heart ached. Smaller than the other boys, and introverted as well, Raymond struggled when it came to socializing. He was her quiet boy. Her shy one. Smart as a whip and wise beyond his years. A touch on the spectrum, but she didn't medicate him. He didn't need it. He just needed more quiet space than the other boys.

More than one night she'd seen him sneak out of the room he shared with his brothers to bunk downstairs on the couch. He didn't fear the dark because her strong Raymond had survived it.

"We got our report cards today. But I kind of lost mine." He nibbled on a cookie, having said his piece and told her without telling her exactly what had happened.

Those damned bullies again.

She wanted to drag him onto her lap and hug him, but Raymond wasn't the type to want to snuggle. Even with his siblings he tended to often stand on the outside looking in.

"Want to talk about it?" Ten years of age, but already way ahead when it came to his schooling, he had a wisdom beyond his years. But emotionally? Still a little boy who had feelings that hurt even as he didn't understand why he cared.

For a second, she thought he wouldn't reply. He managed a soft, "Why does no one like me?"

"Of course, people like you," she huffed. "You

have friends." At least one good friend since kindergarten, who she realized hadn't been around in the last few weeks.

Raymond explained why in his next sentence. "Not anymore. Evan moved."

The news halted her for a second. "I didn't know."

"His mom and dad separated. She took him to Nova Scotia."

"I'm sorry." A trite thing to say to the child who had a hard time making friends.

"It's okay." He lied for her. Her sweet boy. Her heart cracked even more.

"You'll make another friend."

He rolled his shoulders. "No, I won't. The other kids don't like me."

Not entirely true, but with his anxious nature, he believed it. "That's not true. You are plenty likeable. Just ask your family." It sounded stupid, yet what else could she say? "Does Dominick know the boys are picking on you again?" In the past, her oldest child had stepped in.

Raymond shook his head. "No. And don't tell him. He'll get in trouble."

As if Dominick would care. In that moment, she didn't give a damn either. For all people talked about peaceful solutions, sometimes the quickest and easiest way to handle a bully was to sic a bigger threat on them. But she didn't need Dominick to fight to be able to say, "Your brother would gladly accept the consequences if he thought it would help you. And why is that?"

Raymond grimaced. "I see what you did. You're making me say he loves me, ruining my argument that no one likes me."

"What can I say? I enjoy the rare occasion where I get to prove you wrong." Because Raymond seldom made mistakes. A genius being held back by the school system.

"You just proved only family can like me and that's because they have to. Those boys at school hate me." His body sagged, and he had another tiny bite of his cookie.

"I can talk to the school—"

He gave her a horrified glance. "No. Don't. Remember last time?"

At the reminder, she bit back a wince. She'd only wanted to protect him.

"Is there anything I can do?" she asked.

He said nothing, just gave another dejected shrug.

It killed her.

She wanted to march into his school and raise holy hell, but it would make things worse for her sweet boy. Not better. At the same time, she couldn't not act.

The next day, when Raymond came home from school, the knees to his jeans ripped, she asked what happened. He lied and said he tripped.

This couldn't go on, or she'd end up in jail for throttling the bullies.

Despite money being tight, because she had lot of mouths to feed, she went shopping that night. The next day when Raymond came down for breakfast, his face drawn and anxious, she said to him, "You're staying home today."

"I can't. I have a test."

"A test isn't more important than your wellbeing. I think you need a break from school."

"I'll get one in two days on the weekend." He began to grow agitated. Raymond might struggle socially, but academically the boy was a genius.

"Fine. Write your test. But after school, I want us to have a chat."

While he went and aced a quiz, she used that time to finish her arrangements. Then she picked up Raymond and Jessie so they didn't have to take the bus.

Once they got home, Raymond headed for the stairs. Before he could disappear, his face buried in a book, she snared him.

"Can you come here for a second? I got something for you." That something was a second-hand computer and a stack of workbooks.

Raymond stared at it with its fat keyboard, the yellow casing matching that of the monitor, the body of the machine black metal. Not the newest machine on the market, but given she only had two hundred dollars, it would do the trick. She hoped.

When he said nothing, she prodded him. "It's for you. To do your schoolwork on."

His eyes lit with excitement before they dulled. "We can't afford it." Young and yet he knew they had a tight budget.

"Too late. I can't return it. You'll have to keep it."

His brow creased. "But it's not my birthday." And Christmas was still almost two months away.

"This isn't a present. It's so you can study."

"Study what?"

"Anything you like. Take a look."

He sifted the pile of books and cast her a curious glance. "These are school workbooks."

She nodded. "Yes, your grade, plus the next three if you'd like to get ahead. The seller also threw in a book on computer programming."

"I read a book on coding," he observed, moving aside the books to find the one mentioned. He immediately began to flip through it.

Her heart filled with warmth as she softly said, "I got this because I thought we could try home-schooling."

At her words, he froze and glanced at her fully,

his face cautiously hopeful. "No more going to class?"

She shook her head. "Not for the next little bit because we're going to try learning at home. And sometimes at my work so we can save on having a sitter."

He grimaced. "I don't need a babysitter."

According to law he did, even though mentally he was probably more responsible than most adults.

"Someone's got to keep an eye and make sure you work hard," she teased.

"I won't let you down, Mommy." The smile on Raymond's face was worth the strain on her bank account balance.

Not all his siblings were as gracious. Dominick—just turned seventeen—was vocal about his displeasure. "How come he doesn't have to go to school? No fair. I want to stay home, too."

"Then just get suspended again," said Stefan with a snicker.

"You little shit."

"Boys!" Nana raised her voice and they both piped down. Stefan smirked, Dominick glared, Raymond hunched in on himself.

Later that night as she passed their door, open a crack for circulation, she heard Dominick ask his brother, "Who was it this time?"

"Doesn't matter."

"Tell me. I'll kick their ass," Dominick promised.

"I'll help so they don't bug you and you can go to school," Stefan added.

Raymond's reply: "Won't matter. No one likes me."

Her heart cracked and then burst as she heard Dominick whisper, "We like you, dumbass. And anyone who doesn't deserves a knuckle sandwich."

After that, the boys didn't say a word about Raymond being schooled from home. He thrived. She'd worried he'd suffer at the lack of people inter-action, that he'd change. He did, but for the better. He began joining the family more in the evenings and weekends. Even speaking up, which she was glad to see no one made a big deal about.

Her boy relaxed, lost that tenseness of before as he plowed through the books she got him. Passed the tests with ease and scored so high he had to redo them at a school while monitored by a teacher. He aced those as well.

As he got older, he kept moving ahead to the point she couldn't afford the books and got him the internet instead. By fifteen, her boy graduated with honors and got scholarships but stayed local. He did his university while living at home, taking as many online options as he could. After, he got a program-ming job that didn't require commuting and insisted she retire. She'd already gone to part time, as

Dominick and Stefan also insisted on throwing help her way. More than she needed, but none of her boys would take no for an answer.

They'd turned into such fine men, but she still worried about her little Raymond who hated going out and socializing. All his friends were online or related to him.

Raymond only rarely left the house, and even more rarely dated. Nana knew he'd have to get out of the basement one day. The problem being, how to convince him the world—make that people—had something to offer that his machines couldn't?

She wanted him to find love.

1

FIND LOVE ONLINE BY PLAYING A GAME THAT MATCHES YOU to your perfect partner.

The newest pamphlet with its bold claim sat beside the glass dome covering freshly made muffins. Mom might have moved out a few weeks ago, but she kept popping in with the pretext of checking on him.

He appreciated it because were it not for her and his siblings, he'd have no face-to-face human contact. Even his introverted ass realized that wasn't healthy.

Still, despite almost feeling lonely, he had more reason than ever to be chained to his network in the basement. His brothers had been kidnapped not long ago. As in taken to the lab where Raymond and his siblings had been created by some seriously sick fuckers.

Their Dr. Moreau lab might have blown up and all the evidence destroyed, but Raymond couldn't leave their past alone. He didn't dare. There were people out there that remained aware of their existence. Knew he and his siblings weren't entirely human. His family wasn't safe, and while he might lack the brawn of his brother Dominick, or the acerbic wit of Stefan, or the ballsy courage that his sister Maeve enjoyed, he was smart.

While everyone else went on with their lives after the lab responsible for their creation was destroyed, Raymond used his brains for something other than gaming and coding. He began digging into their pasts for the first time ever. He'd never bothered before their secret came out. When Mom said she had no family, he'd believed her. She'd told him and his siblings that they had no parents, that they were abandoned without any clues, and he'd trusted her.

He'd never looked into his family's past. And now that he was trying, he was getting fucking nowhere.

Frustrating as all hell. He was a guy who solved riddles, could hack into anything, find whatever he wanted. If it left an electronic trail. In this case, he had nothing.

The site of their creation—a secret lab that never

officially existed and was never built according to any city permits—had burned to the ground. He couldn't find any of the former employees. He had no names other than the uncle he didn't remember, Johan Philips, who was a blood brother to their foster mother.

Oddly enough, Mom didn't exist either under her maiden name. As if she'd been wiped out, too. It shouldn't have surprised him given what the lab had been up to. After all, his uncle had been the doctor in charge of changing human embryos into something more.

Huanimorphs they called them, animal human mixes. A dumb name. Raymond much preferred the Valley Wolf Pack's term: shifter.

Shifter made what they could do sound more normal, if that were even possible. He had a hard time wrapping his science brain around the fact that his body and skin, his very humanity, could transform literally into something else.

In his case a lynx. A handsome one he thought, not that he let anyone see it, especially after the incident at the barbecue. Someone had spiked the chocolate fountain, and he went furry for the first time.

He remembered nothing about it, which led to him doing a few controlled experiments in the basement where he'd fabricated a steel cage that required fingers to open. Once secured inside, he'd eaten catnip—the dumbest trigger ever—and became a feline.

Furry, four legged, with acute senses. Not that he remembered any of his time in his lynx shape. According to the wolf pack, and his brothers, who were also affected by catnip, the herb acted like a catalyst drug, forcing them to shift, making them literally mindless beasts.

Could shifting be done without the herb?

The wolves said yes. Even Stefan admitted that under duress he'd managed to change. Not Raymond or Dominick, though. As for Tyson, Mom warned them not to encourage the teenager.

Did Raymond care he couldn't shift on demand? Not really. A lynx couldn't play video games or hack secure databases.

But a giant cat could eat his brother when he came pounding downstairs bellowing, "Ray! When was the last time your lily-white butt saw daylight?"

Raymond whirled in his chair and glared at Dominick. With Mom having relocated close to the city, to save on rent, his brother had moved his shit back in with his girlfriend and taken over the master bedroom on the top floor. They were welcome to it. The basement with all the humming computers was Raymond's domain.

But did anyone respect his space? Nope. Look at the piles of laundry on the floor, the heaps growing daily. Stupid machine was broken, and they were waiting on a new one.

"Daylight is overrated," Raymond muttered, whirling back to his screens. They'd multiplied since his brothers were kidnapped. He'd also stepped up his security a thousandfold, installing dozens of hidden cameras around the property, even overhead surveillance to watch for drones.

He'd spent countless hours creating hacks that he tied to certain databases and knowledge streams. He needed to keep a better eye on his family and their new allies, the werewolves. So far, nothing had tripped any of his alarms, but paranoia had ridden him ever since he'd failed to protect his family before.

He should have seen the enemy coming. Never mind the fact he didn't know they were in danger. He wouldn't fail again.

His annoying big brother spun his chair around. "Come on, zombie boy. You need sunshine and fresh air to stay healthy."

The claim brought a snort to Raymond's lips. "UV rays cause skin cancer, and the air in here is filtered to be free of pollen and other pathogens. I have allergies." To pretty much all of nature and dust. For a while he thought he was gluten intolerant, too, but that turned out to be a lactose thing. A kitty who couldn't drink milk. The irony. Good thing these days he could replace the regular stuff with alternatives. He would die without his daily dose of chocolate milk.

"You need to exercise, or your ass won't fit through the door," his brother taunted.

"I get plenty of exercise." He kept weights on his desk and curled them while waiting for his online gaming parties to load. He belonged to a few role-playing worlds. When waiting for a program to execute, he did pushups and sit-ups. He'd learned through trial, ache, and error that sitting too long hurt his body.

"Dude, you are making way too many excuses to stay down here. It's not healthy."

"It's none of your business what I do."

"Fuck yeah it is."

Raymond glared. "Did Mom send you to bug me?"

"Mom didn't have to. You need to get out from inside these walls once in a while."

"I was in the kitchen an hour ago."

Dominick uttered a noise halfway between a snort and a chuckle. "Anywhere inside this property doesn't count."

"I can't leave. I have too much to do." Raymond spun back to his screens to check, even knowing he had notifications set to ensure he wouldn't miss anything.

"No, you don't. You need to let this go." Dominick's tone softened. "What happened to me and Tyson wasn't your fault."

Damn his brother for thinking he could absolve him. "I should have seen it coming."

"None of us could have. We all thought we were normal. How were we supposed to know we were a shaken cocktail made in a lab?" His brother tried to make it a joke.

It fell flat. It was a reminder that their lives were a lie, that their own mother had hidden the truth. And Raymond should have known.

Why hadn't he dug deeper into their past? How could he have not seen the inconsistencies?

He knew the reason why. He'd never ever expected his mom to be a liar.

"I have to do this," he said softly and with a tone that brooked no argument.

A heavy sigh left Dominick. "I know you do. And honestly, I understand the feeling. After Anika got kidnapped"—Anika being Dominick's girlfriend—"I blamed myself. I should have been there. Protected her. When I told her, she ended up smacking me and calling me a few names."

"Only a few?" Raymond had actually heard part of that yelling match.

"The point being, don't let your guilt overtake

you. Would have. Could have. Should have. We can't keep looking back, only forward."

"Exactly. Learn from my mistakes. We won't get caught again."

"Fine. You want to be psycho, be psycho, but I really wish you'd leave the basement. Doesn't have to be for long. I'll even watch your screens if it makes you happy. Go hit a bar, have a few beers. Relax for a couple hours and get laid."

The idea of going out and looking for sex didn't appeal. "I'm not interested in hooking up with a stranger." He didn't need sex that badly. He'd lost his virginity in university. The experience was okay. Since then he'd met up with a few women from the online gaming world, but in-person meetings tended to leave him underwhelmed. Might be why he'd not had sex with anyone other than his hand in a few years. And he was fine with it. He didn't like people getting close.

"Everyone you meet starts as a stranger, dumbass."

The conversation with his brother bored. Raymond would prefer to be gaming. "Stop worrying about me. I'm fine."

"That's debatable," muttered Dominick.

"Don't you have to go to work or something?"

"I just got home. You do realize it's almost five in the afternoon, right?"

Actually, he paid very little attention to time. But he did enjoy one thing. "What's for dinner?" The one good thing about having his brother and his girlfriend living here now that Mom had moved out was they made food and always offered him some.

"You're on your own tonight. Maeve's working late, and I'm taking Annie to dinner." Maeve being their sister who lived there on and off. She'd been spending a lot of time at Mom's, too.

A lack of dinner didn't pose a problem. Raymond ordered himself a shawarma sandwich with garlic potatoes, paid online, and asked for contactless delivery. He loved that most places had kept it in place once the pandemic slipped off to where viruses hid once they'd ravaged the population.

As he waited for his food, he tossed a few lures onto the dark web, subtle requests for information about the project that created him and his siblings. Especially anything pertaining to the man who'd hired their uncle and kidnapped Stefan and Tyson, the mysterious Mr. X.

No one had yet pinged, but Raymond knew how to be patient. While he waited for an alarm to go off, he slid into one of his online personas. The VR glasses fit over his eyes and covered his ears. The gloves he wore would track their movement in the virtual world he entered.

Unlike the movies and their attempt at drama, he

knew what he saw wasn't real, such as the bustling marketplace, designed with a medieval appeal that included lots of wood, pennants, and hawking sellers. It had an old-fashioned appeal without any neon or flashing lights. That was his other game, set in space.

For this particular game node—a fantasy-type epic—he wore the body of a dwarf, about four feet tall, barrel wide, and stupidly strong, but slow. He also had no magic. However, his attributes included an ability to forge weapons that could be sold for large sums, and in a battle, he was the impervious ram that in a berserker rage could rampage through the opposition.

He strode through the market, not really eyeing the wares. He aimed for the guild to see what quests had been posted. He'd just left his last raiding party because of a power struggle between two of the members. He didn't care which prepubescent gamer led them; he just liked the thrill of the quest and the strategy when taking down complex enemies.

Visually, the guild appeared as a stone building, two stories with only thin slits rather than windows. The massive door was guarded by tusked minotaurs who would give pause to anyone thinking to attack or rob the guild. Today, his business didn't require him to go inside. While it might appear solid, if touched, the wall to the left of the entrance would turn into a digital message board showing available tasks.

First a question: *Solo or group?*

Solo. Next query. *Difficulty level?*

The harder the mission, the better the prize or favors he could accumulate. He particularly wanted some get-out-of-jail free passes. While he didn't usually start fights, he never hesitated to throw his avatar into the mix. This particular rule treated the town and its laws like the real world in some respects. Cause trouble, go to jail and pay a fine. Or call in a favor and walk free instead.

Rescuing a princess or prince, depending on sexual preference, came with a supposed marriage and alliance. It also meant a virtual wife, and they could get rather demanding. *Why haven't you gone and conquered the nation next door?* He'd tried being the princess a few times just for shits and giggles, but that led to a whole new slew of issues with the prince. *What do you mean you don't want me to message you? I was going to send you pictures.* Fool him once, shame on him, twice, and he choked as he beheld purple-eyed monster pics.

Dick pics were not cool. He was so traumatized and violated he put a subroutine on his sister's computer that checked messages for penile images. He also usually gave the police tips if the perv's online presence warranted checking into. Raymond might not leave the house often, but he still watched over his family.

He should be working on that task right now, but he needed a break. A mind wipe from all the stress he'd endured lately.

A nice easy quest would do the trick. Something in a cave with a monster that would require him whacking a few minions on his way to the big boss's lair.

As he contemplated between two—mutant rat inside the sewers, which meant mucking in filth, or a troublesome bog wight, also wet and icky—someone in the virtual marketplace moved in close to him and cast a bubble. For those not familiar with this particular term, it meant encasing a party of two or more in a privacy cocoon where no other players could see or hear them. What he didn't know was why.

Raymond turned and beheld a troll avatar, and an odd one. First, it had opted to go with pink rather than green skin. It sported curly white hair on its head and arms. Female judging by the pendulous breasts barely contained by the ivory furred vest. The sunglasses were also wildly out of place. The game didn't usually allow for modern accessories.

The troll held a club over her shoulder and stared down at him.

"Can I help you?" he asked.

"Took your time before showing up."

"I think you have the wrong person," he replied as he turned away and, with a slash of his hand, broke the bubble.

The marketplace noise filled its spot, but he still heard the troll. "I'm not mistaken. You're shorter than expected."

"Whereas you're freakishly tall. Is there a point to this?" He'd learned a long time ago that some people just liked to be twats online. He didn't encourage it.

"I was curious about you."

"Me? We've never met."

"Not in person," the troll admitted, her tone guttural and yet lilting with a strange femininity. "But from what I've discerned, you're interesting."

An odd choice of words. "Don't tell me you're the type to listen to rumors. I'm sure they're grossly exaggerated."

"Are they?" The bubble returned, encasing them in a zone of just two. "Because I heard a lot of interesting stuff about you, Raymond."

2

Raymond froze. The troll had said his name, the real one. He almost jumped out of the game, but hesitated. Who was this person? Could it be someone he knew fucking with him?

A swipe showed the name and stats of the avatar in front of him. Stats set to private, meaning he couldn't see their game level or start date. Nothing. The only thing he was allowed to see was the code name PinkLlama5309.

"Who are you?" he asked.

"Who do you think I am?" The coy reply was at odds with the beast.

"Probably a sixteen-year-old boy with nothing better to do than be annoying. Don't mess with me, little brother." It had to be Tyson, his teenage brother. Raymond had set him up a few online gaming profiles a year ago. The kid hadn't played in months, but he'd know how to find Raymond in here.

"I'm not Tyson. Or any of your other family members," the troll taunted. "But I know all about them, and you, Raymond."

The chill had settled into his bones. It occurred to him to deny, deny, deny. "You have the wrong person," he lied as he then swiped to remove the bubble around them again.

PinkLama5309 didn't stop him from taking it down, but her avatar smiled, showing off its teeth. "You are Raymond Hubbard in Ontario, Canada."

Now he wasn't just scared, he was angry. "And so what if I am? What are you going to do with that information? Dox me? For doing what?" He wasn't an asshole online.

"You know exactly what you're doing, and it will stop. Or the world will find out about you and catnip."

Panic bloomed inside him. "Who are you?" How did they know of his weakness? His deepest secret?

"We've never met. We never will. Because this is your one and only warning, Raymond. Stop what you're doing, or everyone will find out where you came from. You and your siblings," the voice purred.

"We came from a mom and dad who couldn't

keep us," he replied. He wasn't dumb enough to admit anything where it might be recorded.

"We both know that's a lie. You were made in a lab that I helped destroy so that its secrets would die with it. But you just can't leave things alone. You're stirring up trouble. And it needs to stop."

"You're threatening me?"

"Think of this as a friendly warning."

Didn't feel very friendly. At the same time, he was intrigued. He'd been losing hope before this conversation, close to giving up since he couldn't find anything, and now…now he knew he was on the right track.

"Why do you care if I poke? After all, if the secret comes out, then it only affects me and my family."

"Are you seriously that stupid?" PinkLama5309 snapped. "You and your siblings are not the only lives at stake. Stop digging and asking questions, or the next time there won't be a warning." The troll meant that quite literally. She swung the club right at his avatar's head. Totally unexpected, especially since the marketplace was a neutral zone. Also it was against the law, however, in order to break a law. the ability to act had to exist.

His dwarf got knocked aside by the giant club, and then because that wasn't enough, he got pummeled to the point he required a resurrection ritual in a temple. That would cost him.

Raymond hastily jumped out of the VR with a curse. "What the fuck was her problem?"

If it was a her. Could even be a him. An avatar didn't have to reflect anything about its user at all.

But now he was the one who needed to find out more.

Exactly who was this PinkLlama5309? How did they know so much about him? His family.

For fuck's sake, they knew about the lab. Claimed to have helped destroy it.

Didn't that make them allies?

Given what happened, he didn't see them joining forces that easily. Too bad. He wanted to thank Pink-Llama5309 for lifting his flagging spirits. She'd indicated there were more of them out there.

More undiscovered brothers and sisters. Answers, too.

Raymond tossed his VR equipment onto a table. His dinner had arrived while he played. He took a second to reheat it before taking it downstairs.

As he ate, he checked his systems for any messages or pings. Nothing. He kept eating. Using a machine that was set to watch the stock market, he started a search on PinkLlama5309.

Nothing popped up on the net. Which didn't mean shit. Could be the person used that handle only in the game.

Logging in to the game server, he typed the avatar

name in a search function. Blank. It didn't return anything at all. He typed it again, leaving out the numbers.

Still nada.

Was the search function broken?

He typed in blue llama and got a few hundred hits. Pink Llama with a space. Zilch. How curious. As he debated jumping back into the game, he was logged out of it. Weird but not unheard of. Games glitched all the time.

He logged in.

Access denied.

He checked his cap locks. Off. Despite his stuff being saved, he typed his credentials in.

Access denied.

He refreshed his browser.

Still wouldn't let him log in.

Argh!

He went to grab some dessert in the form of ice cream. He tried to not think of his brother's remark about his ass. His ass was fine, and to prove he didn't care, he would eat the entire half-carton of ice cream.

His next log-in worked, and he was inside his profile. He returned to the search menu and typed in PinkLama5309.

No results.

He retried PinkLlama and netted a return of over

one thousand users with that in the name. 5309 had even more hits.

He tapped his lip. Had he misread the name? Possible. Could be they changed it to something completely different. But...he leaned forward in his chair. Even if changed, the history of that character followed, meaning the new name would have been logged as the person who beat the crap out of him in his statistics. He flipped screens to his character's history.

A glance at his character log showed him going straight from the market to the temple. Dead of injuries but no recorded info on how he'd gotten that way.

It was as if he'd met a ghost. Impossible. Even retired characters never fully disappeared.

He poked inside the player hall of fame. He peeked inside some of the chat rooms, looking for PinkLlama. He didn't find a single one.

Out of curiosity, he logged into other gaming worlds he belonged to. Went wandering around. Got into a few online fights out of frustration and completely lost track of time.

Not that time had much meaning to him.

He wasn't a morning person and often kept odd hours. He slept in stints. A few hours here. A few there. Usually shortened because an alert woke him.

He'd handle the notification, check on a few things, eat, then nod off again for a few.

Two days after meeting PinkLlama and no closer to finding that user or anything about the lab, he was awake when the text arrived in the middle of the night. It was addressed to him by his full name, and not his handle. It dropped into his mailbox on the dark web.

Raymond read it and arched a brow.

Raymond Isaiah Hubbard, I told you to stop poking. Last warning. Or else. Signed, *PinkLlama.*

He blinked. The mystery troll had returned and thought they could threaten him?

He replied. *Or else what?* Because any poking that caused a warning deserved even more attention in his books.

The reply came in the form of a full system shutdown, the kind that wiped his machines so that the only thing that appeared on his screen every time he rebooted was a pink llama wearing sunglasses and a grin.

Impossible. Yet not, apparently. Someone had managed to trace him back and then hack through his firewalls.

It fired his anger. Ignited his need for retaliation. Roused his curious kitty.

Game on.

3

PinkLlama—aka Lainey Smith—signed off, sort of. She never fully switched anything off. She knew better than to stop watching what happened in the world and online. Her existence depended on staying ahead of trouble. She preferred to avoid it if possible and never got involved.

Until lately.

No longer was she content to just electronically watch. She'd finally begun to meddle, which was why she didn't appreciate Raymond Hubbard of Ottawa, Canada, charging around online making a lot of noise that would draw attention.

Nosy guy. Sloppy, too. His hacking skills, while decent, lacked the finesse she'd honed. Then again, he probably hadn't gotten the same education she had.

She almost smiled as she imagined his reaction when he realized she'd wiped his servers clean. She'd warned him, and he ignored it. To be nice, she had given him a second warning, and he sassed her in reply.

He totally deserved what happened next. Raymond Hubbard needed a harsh lesson in meddling, not to mention that crashing his systems would give her the time she needed to wipe his sloppy traces.

The idiot had no idea of the lengths she'd gone to in order to rid the world of any mention of the huanimorph project. She'd done her best to protect them. All of them, even those she'd never met.

He thought he and his siblings were so special. They were the lucky ones. They'd gotten out while young. Others weren't as lucky.

She'd only barely escaped, and it was a plan months in the making. She'd subtly layered some code within programs as she dealt with the tasks given to her by her handlers. Given how closely they watched her every move, she couldn't overtly act. She knew what happened to rebels. They disappeared and were never heard of again.

Lainey's careful planning paid fruit. She set in motion a cascading series of events that led to her escaping her creators, her captors. Once she hit the real world, she went into deep hiding to ensure they had no way of finding her. She wouldn't be captured again. But even more than that, she feared they wouldn't let her live.

I know too much. And a weapon was only good if controlled. Unfortunately for them, Lainey wasn't in the mood to be anyone's puppet anymore.

And she wasn't content to remain hidden. The huanimorph project had to be destroyed, starting with the hidden labs. One by one, she'd taken them out. She destroyed the European one first, then the one in South America. She left the Canadian one, the place she was born, for last.

As to how she did it? Where there was access, she could play, and destroy.

So many companies these days relied on machines to control things. Heating. Cooling. Power loads. Even better, more and more of them were also managing those functions via networks. Once she gained control, it proved easy to overheat the servers and turn off safety measures on other systems, which caused a few explosions.

Kaboom. No more evil lab. No more doctors and machines. And the evidence of what they'd done? Up in smoke because the paranoid Mr. X didn't allow information off site.

Lives were lost. Some probably innocent. But the ones she'd saved were worth the cost to her soul.

Still, she worried. Despite the original labs and

notes being destroyed, not everyone who knew about the huanimorph project had died. Scientists and Mr. X remained aware of their existence. And then there were the other escapees, who could become a problem. The Hubbards weren't the only ones who'd managed to get out, although they'd been the youngest at the time of their escape.

Lainey had located others since her own departure, and even discovered the original subjects of the huanimorph project: four actual werewolves. Real ones that changed into wolves and everything. One had died of testing, one of suicide, and the third was taken out for attacking staff. One of them did manage to get out, though.

As for the one vampire the Xlabs had in custody? It resulted in a fourth lab in the Antarctic being sealed shut. According to the short message she'd discovered before destroying the lab in Europe, the vampire in custody battled past the drugs and infected the minds of those working there. Not that anyone reported it. Surveillance footage showed the staff going crazy and killing each other. Then the grin of the vampire that bellowed in rage when the lockdown entombed it and the fire that swept through the vents killed it.

Werewolves. Vampires. It made her wonder if there were more out there she didn't know about.

The moneyman, the mysterious Mr. X, might

have a fifth or even sixth lab out there. One that was better guarded. He definitely had the money to hire assassins and guards and hide where even she couldn't follow. But she kept trying. So long as Mr. X lived, none of the huanimorphs would be safe.

Lainey set off some subroutines and left her computer room, which was basically a bedroom with the windows blacked out. Heading downstairs, she entered the main living area and stretched. When was the last time she'd slept properly? A while. Wouldn't be the first time she forgot to take care of herself, but she didn't have a choice but to work hard.

Freedom came with a price, but also the best kind of perks like hot chocolate, Pop-Tarts, and someone special in her life.

Entering the kitchen, Lainey beamed as she sang, "Morning, sunshine," to the love of her life.

4

"Wakey-wakey, sunshine!" Dominick bellowed.

Startled awake, Raymond almost fell out of his chair. He definitely had to wipe some drool from his face as he realized he'd passed out while working. At least the keyboard wasn't stuck to his cheek again.

"What the fuck?" he grumbled, easing his aching body from the seat.

"I need you to get up." Dominick clapped his hands.

"More like go to bed. I had a long night." He'd not slept since his computers went down. More than forty-eight hours of trying to recover his programs and he wasn't even halfway there.

"Too bad, so sad. It's an emergency."

"What?" The word had him straightening. "Did something happen?"

"Kind of." Dominick fidgeted. "Anika's pregnant."

"That's great!" Then he saw his brother's somber expression. "Shit, what happened? Is there something wrong with the baby?" It was certainly possible given Nimway, Stefan's wife, had recently miscarried.

"We don't know, and that's where the problem starts. Mom says we can't go to a regular doctor on account of me."

Despite having just woken up, Raymond's mind instantly made the connection. "Because the baby has your genetics and we don't know what that means."

His brother paced, anxious, even a bit scared. "What if the baby isn't normal and the doctor sees that?"

"This isn't the movies where they call some secret government number and she's taken away. They'll most likely assume it's a birth defect." Raymond had no way of knowing for sure.

"A kitten inside her belly is more than a defect," lamented Dominick, whose shifted shape was a panther. "What if the baby hurts Annie? She's not like me. Us. She's human. The baby could harm her."

A good point. They had no idea what to expect.

"What did Mom suggest? She is a nurse. She must have connections."

"She told me to sit tight while she figures something out. But I can't." Dominick raked his fingers through his hair.

"Did you talk to Stefan about it?" Their brother, few years younger than Dom, might not know the answer, but his girlfriend, a werewolf, might.

"I spoke to him. He called me a dumbass for not being more careful."

"And what did Nimway say? Did he talk to her about it?"

Dominick grimaced. "She said they use regular doctors because they're not puppies in the womb."

"Can't we assume the same for your child?"

"Can we?"

There was so much they didn't know, and that was why Raymond had ignored PinkLlama's warning. His family needed answers.

Raymond rubbed his face. "What do you need me to do?"

"I don't know." Dominick continued to pace, his big body tense with agitation. "Mom says an ultrasound will show us what's going on inside."

"A machine is easy to borrow, but we need a technician. I wonder if the Pack has someone we can use." Raymond pinched his chin.

"If they don't? Then what? We can't have someone seeing something they shouldn't."

"You're probably panicking for nothing."

"Am I? How do we know for sure? Annie's pregnant. One month at most. She shouldn't even be showing yet, but her belly is popping, and she's puking her guts out daily. It's not normal."

"Says who?"

"Every fucking thing I've read about pregnancy," his brother growled. For a second his eyes flashed, and Raymond's hackles rose in reply at the aggression.

He tamped down the response. "Calm down. I'll figure something out." But it occurred to him that more than ever he needed answers, and he didn't have time to let pride stand in his way. Which was why he posted a very public plea on the dark web, using his phone, the only thing still working.

PinkLlama. I need your help.

A day went by with no reply. He did searches on pregnancy. Even ventured out of the basement at dinner to see Anika for himself. Having not eyed her belly much before, he didn't see the massive difference his brother boasted of, but he did see her suddenly turn green during the meal and run for the bathroom. Poor Dominick gave his plate a mournful look before joining her to offer sympathy.

Raymond went back downstairs and sent another message.

PinkLlama. Will do anything.

He half expected to be ignored.

Instead he got an unexpected reply. *Anything?*

He didn't even hesitate.

Yes.

5

Lainey knew better than to reply; however, she couldn't ignore Raymond's cry for help, especially since she'd been monitoring his online searches. Pregnancy, both animal facts and human ones. Obviously, Raymond had knocked up a girl and now panicked about it. With good reason given his genetics.

She would have given him aide no matter what, but she never passed up a good opportunity. In this case, she could use him to access a place she couldn't. Despite messaging via the deep web, she knew better than to leave a texting trail. She knew where she could talk unfettered.

Meet me in the Stagnant Grove.

A location in the game that few gamers bothered with. The water ate most armor, making it expensive to quest in unless you were thick skinned. Like a troll.

Despite it being a quiet location, once Raymond arrived in a new avatar, she added a bubble.

"Is that supposed to impress me?" she asked, referring to the fact he'd come as a troll with golden, tiger-striped, leathery skin and impressive tusks.

"You already know I'm a scrawny basement dweller. Is there a point?"

Was he puny as he claimed? His driver's license with its awful picture had him at six foot, one hundred and eighty pounds. Slim, but not too skinny. She'd failed to find any other pictures. He must have wiped them purpose. A guy who liked his privacy. She could respect that.

"Gotta ask, with a handle like PinkLlama, why the troll?"

"Because no one is scared of a llama. Duh." She rolled her eyes, not that he could see in the game or real life. She wore sunglasses again.

"You think a pink troll is frightening?"

"You tell me. Your dwarf is still being resurrected." She flashed a toothy grin.

He grimaced, his tusks jutting even further. "And it's costing me a fortune. But not why I reached out. I need your help."

"Because you got someone pregnant." She wondered who. He didn't have close female contacts other than his sister and mother. Maybe one of his brothers' girlfriends? Was he the type to do that kind of thing?

"Me?" His jaw dropped, impressively cartoonishly low. "I didn't knock anyone up. My brother did."

"Which one?"

"Dominick."

"Hmm." All she said, but he jumped on it.

"What's that mean?"

"Just that Stefan and his werewolf girlfriend are less likely to have issues."

"What kind of issues?" As his panic heightened, and his avatar began to drool, she held up a hand.

"Slow down. You'll get answers, but first, you have to do something for me."

Even in virtual reality she could sense his agitation. "What do you want?"

"Nothing too hard or horrible."

"Then why not do it yourself?" he snapped.

"Because I'm unable to leave for overnight trips."

"I have to go somewhere?" he almost bellowed.

While not currently clinically declared agoraphobic, Raymond did have intense introvert tendencies. She couldn't exactly criticize though, because she was just as home-bound, only not for the same reasons.

"Yes, you have to go somewhere. Good news is

you're close enough to drive or fly, so you could technically make it a day trip."

"When I said I'd do anything, I didn't mean murder. I am not an assassin."

"You wouldn't kill to help your family?" Because she would and not lose any sleep over it.

"I…" He hesitated. "I'd like to say no, but I really don't know what I'd do to keep them safe."

"If it's any consolation, there should be no killing involved."

"Does that include me not being taken out?" he asked.

"The worst that might happen is you could get arrested. But only if you get caught. I don't recommend it."

"Obviously," he snorted. "Fine. What do I have to do?"

Her troll avatar grin was something borderline nightmare-inducing as she said, "You need to deliver a package."

6

On the surface what PinkLlama asked appeared simple. Get on a plane and fly to Toronto or make the four-hour road trip, five if he stuck to speed limits. At Union Station, where trains and buses departed at all hours of the day, was a locker with a package and instructions.

Raymond sweated the entire drive down in the minivan he'd borrowed from his mom. Bobblehead Darth Vader danced on the dash, the suction cup holding him in place. The antics usually helped with his anxiety when he left the house. Nothing could help him now, not even his CBD vape pen.

He couldn't even pinpoint what stressed him the most. There were too many stressors to count.

First, he'd left the house. As in off the property, driving even farther.

Then there was the lack of connection to his network of computers. All he had was his phone, watch, and a laptop in the back that could be wiped remotely if things went to hell.

He really hoped nothing went wrong.

But his mind couldn't help but run through so many scenarios, from suddenly being chased down on the highway to being pulled over by a cop and getting a ticket that would raise his insurance. It would also link him to the road to Toronto if shit went awry.

What was in this supposed package he had to deliver? PinkLlama never said. He knew so little still, like was PinkLlama a woman or a man? Adult, child? Friend, or foe?

He lacked the time to find out. So he took a chance and followed his gut, which said they were on the same side.

Having scouted the area beforehand, Raymond parked on a street where the meters accepted cash and there were no cameras. Then he walked a few blocks to Union Station.

He hunched his shoulders as he entered, his ball cap drawn low over his forehead, probably making himself appear more suspicious than needed, but he couldn't help himself. Cameras watched everything these days, especially busy travel hubs.

He longed to be out of sight and, because of his

haste, went past the area for the lockers and had to turn around. Once he found the right one, he fumbled the combination lock. By the time he retrieved the duffel bag and made it back to the minivan with time to spare on the parking meter, he'd sweated through his T-shirt and hoodie.

How did his brother Dominick handle the stress of missions when he was in the military? His heart raced a mile a minute, fully aware he remained far from home.

Opening the bulky package, the instructions were simple. Assume the identity of a cable man. A collared shirt, company identification, and equipment bag were inside the duffel along with magnets to stick to the van, one for the side with the name of the cable company and a pair to slap over the plates to mask them—a precaution he appreciated. At two o'clock in the afternoon, he should present himself at a building on Queen Street downtown to deal with an internet outage.

Wait, how did she know there'd be an outage? This was like something out of a movie. Or a video game. With that thought on the brain, he remained hyper alert for an attack on the way to the office building, constantly watching his mirrors. No stunt drivers on motorbikes came blasting from an alley. No dark-colored trucks surrounded him and started shooting.

It felt too easy.

As he parked around the corner—for extra discretion—the skin on his nape prickled. *Am I being watched?*

A casual scan from side to side as he sauntered down the street, toolbox in hand, didn't show anyone watching. Only as he neared the main doors did a dark sedan pull to the curb. A group of people emerged, and Raymond ducked his head, pretending interest in his phone, like every other stranger on the sidewalk. So many people.

He hated the city. The lack of privacy. Being noticed.

The car pulled away, and he entered a medical facility that featured all kinds of doctors. Foot. Eye. Physio. Including a floor for fertility.

A security guard spotted him and, hitching his belt, said, "About time you got here. Everyone is losing their shit because the internet is down."

"That's what I'm, uh, here to fix," Raymond mumbled then cleared his throat to add, "I'll just, uh, need to see your equipment room."

The guard didn't even ask for identification, just led the way to the basement, complaining the whole way about the upper floors being snotty about something he couldn't control. As if it was his fault the internet went out. Fucking entitled pricks.

Raymond nodded but said nothing as the guard

led him to a room humming with machines. He felt overdressed from the heat radiating. Definitely the right place.

"Guess I'll get started." He moved to the spot on the wall where the work order claimed the cable box could be found. The black metal square had a lock. A glance over his shoulder showed the guard watching, meaning he had to dig for the special key that was supposed to keep these boxes tamper free.

Click. The lid popped open. and then he had to fake checking cables with a voltmeter. Useless really. But the guard appeared satisfied because he left Raymond alone.

About time. There wasn't much left to do. Just stick a small device the side of a pea to any of the fiber cables. It wouldn't be easily noticed.

Especially as it sprouted legs and climbed.

Raymond blinked. Exactly what had he unleashed?

Did it matter? He was done. Easy peasy, lemon squeezy as his mom would say.

Too easy.

He kept expecting someone to yell after him as he left. For his arm to be grabbed and someone to demand he come with them. Despite the stress and the sweat, he made it to the minivan without any problems. He dumped all the cable guy stuff into a dumpster in Scarborough on his way out of town.

As he drove home, he texted a coded number.

Done.

In return he got a name and address with the word, *Ultrasound*. He immediately forwarded it to Dominick.

Within ten minutes, his brother replied, *Is that a fucking joke? Because it's not fucking funny.*

Frowning, Raymond pulled over. Rather than ask his brother what the problem was, he did a search on the info PinkLlama had given him.

When the search result came up, he cursed and then sent another message to the coded number.

What the fuck? I thought we had a deal.

PinkLlama: *You asked for help for the pregnant woman. I gave you the name of a doctor.*

A vet. Which his brother thought was a rude dig.

PinkLlama: *John knows how to handle our kind.*

Our kind. A word slip that had him huffing out a breath.

Holy fuck. PinkLlama was one of them.

7

LAINEY KNEW SHE'D FUCKED UP THE SECOND after she hit Send. No way would a smart guy like Raymond ignore the use of the word "our." He'd start asking questions. Which was fine. He could ask all he wanted. She didn't have to reply.

To her surprise he didn't send anything but, *Thanks.*

Thanks?

She should have been pleased. Instead, she gnawed on her thumb. Would that be the end of it? Or should she remind him he needed to lay low and stop poking?

She couldn't keep cleaning up his messes. She'd gone out of her way to help him even as he increased the risk of discovery. A part of her hated him and his family with their attempt at normal lives. Didn't they know they should hide? What would happen if they were caught?

Never mind the fact they'd escape notice for decades. Now that they'd surfaced they had to be careful. Not do anything to draw attention.

You mean like stalk a guy through a video game and then take down his network? She could have handled him anonymously, screwed with his life in a way that distracted him from his search, and yet she hadn't. She'd chosen to openly involve herself.

Why?

Had she suddenly forgotten her own rules? Did she want to be caught?

Of course not. She'd fought too hard to get where she was. Off grid. Living the good life. She had everything she needed plus a few backup plans in case shit went downhill fast.

Her only goal was to keep the one person she loved safe. Even if it meant shoving other people under the bus.

She monitored Raymond's computer. It had come back online in the most basic fashion and then did nothing. Had he heeded her warning?

She had no way of finding out. He'd not been using his phone either. And if he was talking to his siblings, he did it in a way she couldn't read or hear online. The little fucker. Now that he knew she was watching, he'd ghosted her.

Well played.

She increased her surveillance on his family, even managing to tap into their phones' receivers. People had no clue to the fact the devices listened at all times in case their owners had a command to give. They recorded everything. Every single word or sound uttered. And since it was software, it could be hacked.

His brother Dominick was in a better mood since he'd taken his girlfriend to see John. John—a former doctor for Xlabs, who'd faked his own death and then got cosmetic surgery to change even further— had become a vet. She'd found *John* by accident.

Running into him that first time about four years after her escape, she would have never realized she knew him. The changes were so well done. No more glasses. Shaved head. Earring. Sporting bright colors and a beard. She would have passed right on by if John hadn't gasped.

No mistaking the pallor on his face as he muttered, "Baby fucking jeezus riding a unicorn, it's you."

That expression. She knew it. She remembered John. Only that wasn't his name before.

She stared and offered a cold smile. "Yes, it is me. Sorry you recognized me."

He must have seen his death in her gaze because he stammered, "Don't kill me. Please. I left because I couldn't handle what they were doing."

"Says you."

"Says the fact they'd kill me if they ever found out I was alive."

"Cry me a river." She wasn't about to get soft. John posed a liability.

"Listen, I've changed. I swear. I help animals now."

Wrong thing to say. *"Because we're animals to you."*

"No!" he hotly denied. *"I want to heal, not hurt. I never wanted to hurt anyone."*

She couldn't have said what possessed her to trust him that day. Maybe a sense of loneliness given she didn't trust anyone. The fact she needed an ally.

John lived and proved useful over the years. He even became a friend. He let her know that Dominick's girlfriend was pregnant with twins, hence the rapid growth of her belly. Both human-appearing thus far. They would closely monitor her progress. In the meantime, mom and dad were giddy and kept repeating, "Holy shit, twins."

Their awe brought out her protective instinct. She had to keep the Hubbards safe. They seemed like good people. Living the life. Loving.

But where was Raymond?

A third day passed, and he'd not posted a damned thing. Impossible. He had to be doing something that involved the internet. He must have found a way to hide it.

Jerk had more talent than she'd given him credit for.

While she kept an eye open for Raymond, she checked in on the bug he'd planted. It was actually the second half of a two-part system. The first item involved a camera in the elevator. Disguised within a button that made to appear as if it belonged on the elevator's panel, it recorded every time someone got in.

But to hide its presence, it didn't have an outgoing signal until the cab lowered to the basement level. Once there, it sent a quick burst of information to the receiver, the tiny robot that clung to the fiber cables then attached itself to an outgoing email or file transfer outside the building network and bounced to a few nodes before coming home to Lainey.

Complicated? Very, because Lainey knew better than to be sloppy. She used to work for the Xlabs, unwillingly of course. She knew all the tricks and had long ago spotted the holes in their surveillance network. Despite seeing, she never did anything to fix them. She knew one day she might need those flaws.

She was hoping to catch footage of Mr. X on her camera. She'd traced the in vitro company on the fifth floor to a shell company that belonged to him. All the evidence she'd gathered pointed to it.

If she could get a clear facial profile, she might finally be able to track Mr. X. Match a name to the voice. Figure out who the mystery man was. No one ever saw him except staff. Patients of the labs only ever heard his voice. She'd asked John what Mr. X looked like, and his reply was, "A decent-looking anyone man." Non-descript, always dressed in a suit, a touch over six feet, fit and sporting a full head of hair that changed color and style with each visit. He also wore a mask. A seemingly impermeable shield of metal that dully gleamed. No features at all to be discerned, not even a strap holding it in place. Glued in place, as if he had no face.

Doubtful. More like Mr. X was paranoid about being recognized. He could be anyone. She wouldn't know unless he spoke to her.

And even then, what if the timbre of his voice changed?

She had to see his face. Know the enemy. Hence the cameras in the places he might appear. A building in downtown Toronto would take note of someone wearing a metal mask in the daytime. The pandemic and the face coverings might have lingered among some in the population, but none of those covered the eyes.

As she waited for a hit, she spent time with her love. Tidied the house. Fetched some fresh food. Monitored her scans.

Still nothing from Raymond.

On the fourth day after he planted the bugs she got a knock on her door.

Unexpected given she never had visitors. Nor did she have any deliveries scheduled. But most surprising of all? None of her alarms had gone off.

Her watch didn't vibrate a warning. The screen attached to her doorbell by the front door remained dark as if no one were there.

Lainey glanced upstairs. She needed to handle this quietly. She grabbed the nearest rifle—she had more than a few stashed—and went to the thick, solid wood door and pressed her ear to it. Had she misheard?

Knock. She stumbled back. Another rap and then a distinctly masculine, "I know you're in there. Are you going to answer? It's cold outside."

"Then go away." She didn't know who it was. Why was her camera stuck on a loop? How had she been hacked?

"I can't leave. We need to talk."

Her heart stopped. It couldn't be. "Who the fuck are you?"

"It's Raymond. Raymond Hubbard. I need to talk to Pink Llama."

8

RAYMOND STOOD OUTSIDE THE THICK wooden door, fighting for patience. His arrival was probably a shock, but then again, PinkLlama had to have known she'd fucked up.

Knowing PinkLlama was like him made him understand her better. He knew why she'd come after him, and it wasn't to personally piss him off. She'd thought she was protecting them.

Awesome, if he'd been a fucking child. He might not come out of his basement often, but he wasn't an idiot or a complete coward. He didn't need someone taking care of his problems. However, the intellect in him wanted answers to his questions.

He'd managed to glean some from John, a burly fellow that he kept an eye on during the ultrasound done on Anika at John's veterinary practice.

He'd had them come in with a pet to make it look legit. Meaning they were now the proud owners of a dog. The tiniest dog in creation, Dominick declared.

But Anika wanted something she could put in her lap and snuggle, and Dom couldn't say no. So their little fluffy handful went with them to the vet, where they saw two babies inside of Anika but not much else yet at this stage. Two blobs of cells and yet his brother almost cried.

John didn't ruin that happy moment. He held Raymond back when Anika ran to find a bathroom and Dominick followed to hold her hair.

Quickly John had whispered, "It's too soon yet to tell if the fetuses will take."

"Wait, what? Something is wrong?" Raymond had gasped.

"We won't be able to tell until the second trimester. That's when the weird shit can happen."

"You're telling me she could have, um, er"—he sought a word that wouldn't insult and settled for—"complications?"

"Yes. Which is why it's good she came here early."

"What happens if, um, the complication materializes?"

"To save the mother, we have to terminate the fetus."

He winced. "Oh shit. I don't know if they'd agree to that."

"Then there would be a strong chance she'd die."

No wonder John didn't tell Dominick or Anika. Let them worry about it if it became an issue.

"Anything else I should know, Doc?" he'd asked.

Turned out, John had plenty to say, except about PinkLlama. When questioned, the guy clammed up. Raymond tried pushing and got a terse, "Leave Pink alone. Trust me, she's not a person you should mess with."

She? One more clue. "She started it," was his petulant reply as he sought to play dumb for more info.

"Doesn't matter who started it. She will end you if she thinks you pose a danger."

Going out on a limb, Raymond stated, "She's one of us."

John looked entirely too grave as he said, "No, she's not, and you'd best remember that."

What did that mean? Was it because she wasn't a feline like Raymond and his brothers? So what? Some of his siblings had different animals; it still connected them.

Could it be that like Raymond she was anxious? Afraid of being caught? But what if they worked together? She couldn't be all bad. After all, she'd let John, a former doctor, live.

Raymond became determined to find her, but he had to be subtle. She'd outsmarted him thus far. Just look at his computers. Scrap metal for the most part. It would take weeks to reprogram everything. She'd even corrupted his backups.

But he had one ace up his sleeve.

The laptop that he used when he had to leave the house but worried about being robbed. It gave him the access he needed without leading to his actual identity. He couldn't let PinkLlama know he was coming.

Rather than search everywhere, he narrowed his focus to where they'd first met. In the game. The fact she'd had the sunglasses and managed to wipe her traces meant she had a backdoor inside. Possibly a hacker, but what if the fact she knew the game and could manipulate it indicated a deeper knowledge? Could it be something as simple as PinkLlama being one of the original software coders?

He'd not expected that theory to pan out. And yet, when he dug into the game, and the crew who built it, he encountered an article with a picture of three grinning guys. He was reading it over a bowl of cereal in the kitchen just as his sister Maeve walked by.

She pointed. "Why you reading about the douchenozzles?"

"Why the hate?" he asked, noticing she'd

changed her purple streaks to turquoise. Maeve changed colors as often as outfits.

"Because they keep doing these interviews about how they built the greatest online game."

"They kind of did." Something like a billion users would agree.

"Except they keep basking in all the credit when it's a known fact their heaviest lifter on the project is a woman."

He almost choked on his spoonful of cereal. "Do you know her name?"

"No, because she insisted on anonymity. And the only reason anyone ever found out she even existed is because some feminist group got all pissy about the women and how they were portrayed in their world, which is when the douchenozzles paraded out the fact a woman had actually designed them."

Searching up the story didn't net him much information he could use, but the company couldn't hide who it was paying from the IRS. Getting into those records cost him big time since he had to bribe someone for help.

But he ended up getting a name. Lainey Rose. Current age twenty-seven. Single. Living in Alaska of all places. He didn't dare search any deeper.

He wanted to surprise her, which was why he just showed up at her door. He suffered the biggest shock instead.

For one, she wasn't anything close to an eight-foot troll like the avatar in the game. On the contrary, the petite female barely reached his chin. Her hair was platinum with a pink streak. Her skin was smooth without blemish, her eyes covered by wide, dark sunglasses.

"Hi." He remembered his manners.

"Don't you 'hi' me. How did you find me?" she snapped.

"IRS really needs to upgrade their security."

Lainey AKA PinkLlama scowled. "They don't have this address."

"No, they don't. That address is for someone else who forwards your mail to a postal box in Anchorage."

"I haven't checked it in over a week. I pay for it in cash so they don't know where I live," she stated.

That was when he noted one hand held a rifle pointed at the floor.

"Yeah, that almost stumped me, but lucky for me, you pay your property taxes, and while you opted for paperless documents, your postal box is still attached to the account." He'd been rather proud of that bit of sleuthing.

She seemed less than impressed as she glared. "Get out."

"But I just got here." He glanced at the log cabin, which made it sound small and quaint. On the contrary, the home with its very peaked roof stood two stories tall. With the wide-open space inside, it definitely didn't feel cramped or gloomy despite the fact all the windows were shuttered.

It also oozed warmth, which a November in Alaska lacked.

"Can I come in?" he asked, his jacket meant for an Ontario fall, not a northern one.

"No." She went to slam the door.

It occurred to him to put his foot in the crack, but it wasn't just the gun in her hand that gave him pause. He'd not come here to fight but for answers. It wouldn't set the right tone if he started an altercation. So he let her close the door and then knocked. "I know you're listening. I'm not here to cause trouble."

"Then go away."

"I can't. I meant what I said. I need help."

"I already gave you John."

"Which is appreciated. Very much. The babies are fine so far, by the way."

"I know."

Of course, she did. "Why do hate me?" he blurted out without meaning to.

"I don't hate you."

"Have you read the definition to be sure?"

"Fine. I don't like you. You're annoying me."

"I wouldn't if you'd just answer some questions."

"I can't help you."

"I disagree. You know about our past."

"There is no 'our.'" The door opened onto her angry expression. "You and I are nothing alike."

"Were you created in a lab?"

She pursed her lips.

"I already know you were."

"Fucking John."

"Actually"—he grinned—"you just admitted it."

"Asshole." Her lips pinched.

"Takes one to know one."

"We might have both suffered a similar origin story, but that's the only thing we have in common. You and your siblings escaped and got a chance at a normal life."

"We didn't escape. We were rescued from death. And normal kind of went out the window the first time we changed after munching catnip."

"Stay away from it and you'll be fine."

"We are not fine. We need answers."

"Find them somewhere else. I'm not an encyclopedia." She went to shut the door again.

Desperate, he blurted out, "You keep saying we're not alike." And he could tell just by her scent, unlike anything he'd ever smelled. "What are you?"

She opened her mouth, and he didn't know what she would have said if a small voice hadn't said, "Mama? Who dat?"

9

WITH THE ARRIVAL OF HER CHILD, LAINEY lost the window she had to shoot Raymond Hubbard. Damn him tracking her down. He'd seen her biggest secret. Her weakness. The love she would protect at all cost.

She should have shot him the moment she opened the door. Now she'd have to be subtle about it so Sunshine didn't ask questions. After all, Lainey had been teaching her girl how to behave around people since she couldn't have her mingling with the regular public. And she'd expressly explained killing people was bad— unless mommy was protecting her baby girl. Then Lainey could be more cold-blooded than any creature.

"Go to your room, baby girl, while Mommy deals

with this." She turned her back on him to address her daughter.

Sunshine sat on the upper part of the staircase, knees drawn up, toes peeking from the hem of her nightgown. Her long hair remained bound in the fat braid she wore for sleeping. It made for less tears during the daily brushing. Lainey kept offering to shorten it, but Sunshine wouldn't let her cut it. Only the barest of trims was allowed.

"Hello there." Leaning around Lainey, Raymond offered Sunshine a wave and a smile.

Daylight spilled into the house, and since it was too late now to get rid of him, she offered a grumbling invite. "Get inside. We're losing all the heat." She stepped from the door to give him space to enter. He might not be as big as some guys she'd met, but in her house, knowing what he could represent to the wellbeing of her child, he seemed huge.

He entered—she could tell by the shiver down her spine—and she snapped, "Close the door."

He hastily complied.

She returned the unused rifle to the umbrella stand she kept it in. Sunshine knew better than to play with it yet, at the same time, had been taught how to disarm and even shoot it. At five, she was old enough to learn how to protect herself.

Since Sunshine's birth, Lainey had been instilling a sense of self-preservation in her daughter. She would always be hunted. And Lainey might not always be around.

Heading for the staircase, Lainey only had to climb three steps before she reached out to a butt-scooching Sunshine. The familiar slight body came into her arms, smelling of a flowery soap and sugar. Sunshine loved her sweets. Lainey hugged her close. She never missed a chance to show her affection. Had showered her with it from the moment she was born.

Just because Lainey hadn't known it in her life didn't mean she wasn't capable of learning how to feel.

How to love.

Out of habit, she maneuvered her daughter onto her hip only to feel her wiggle.

"Down, Mama. I say hi," demanded her girl.

Lainey nuzzled her and whispered, "What have I said about saying hi to strangers?" The times her daughter encountered people, she knew to keep quiet and close. When night mostly prevailed, they sometimes went into the city and spent a few days at a hotel and did normal things like seeing movies, eating out, and visiting kids' party places, where she did her best to not snatch Sunshine and run.

Sunshine's squeals of excitement didn't draw undue attention. She was just as grabby and giggly as the next child, yet Lainey couldn't help but worry she somehow stood out. At the same time, she knew better than to make her a prisoner for life. The solution couldn't be worse than the dilemma.

"I knows him." Sunshine glanced shyly at Raymond, who made a show of looking around her house. Good thing. He missed Lainey's shocked expression.

It took her a moment before she could recover and say lightly, "Don't be silly. You can't know him because we've never met him before."

At the claim, Raymond turned around and arched a brow. "Not in person, no." He focused on Sunshine and held out his hand. "We haven't been introduced. I'm Raymond. Ray for short."

"Sunshine 'cause Mommy says I'm bright," her daughter lisped adorably. The brightest thing in the world, which meant all Lainey's motherly instincts were going nuts at having this man in her house.

"You're being a little chatterbox today. We're not supposed to tell strangers our secrets," she reminded.

Rather that look chagrinned at the rebuke, Sunshine wiggled hard enough that Lainey set her down. "Dat da man in my picture." Sunshine pointed to the drawing on the fridge, held up by alphabet magnets spelling her name.

Even without looking, Lainey knew what image Sunshine spoke of. Drawn only days ago, it depicted

Lainey and Sunshine holding hands, with her daughter in the middle also gripping the hand of a stick figure man. When Lainey had asked who that was, Sunshine had said, "It's a secret." Then giggled.

Dammit. She should have paid more attention. Asked more questions.

Grumpy and needing some caffeine to take off the edge, she waved a hand at him. "Take off your shoes and have a seat." Turning her back on Raymond, she headed for the kitchen, dimly lit, the shutters all closed. From the outside, no one could see in. She relied on cameras to spot any movement. Cameras that had failed her.

Given all her failsafes, it should have been impossible for him to sneak up on her. She glanced at her kid who held out her hands to take Raymond's coat and staggered under the weight of the Sherpa-lined lumber jacket. Not exactly what she'd imagined him wearing.

Then again, she'd never expected to meet him at all. Yet here he was. And her cameras were still not working. She sent a command to reboot the entire system.

"Need a hand with that?" she heard him ask Sunshine.

"I needs a boost." A rustle of fabric and her daughter chirped, "Thank you." Then she added, "Shoes. Mommy hates dirt."

She didn't hate it outside. But inside, where she spent most of her time, yes, she liked it clean.

"You have a nice house," he said to Sunshine. The first floor of her cabin had an open plan. Only the closet and full bathroom were enclosed. Upstairs, the loft was split into two large bedrooms.

Lainey headed behind the counter for the stove. This time of year, she kept the wood-burning part of it going all the time and just needed to give it a bit more air to get it heating enough to boil water in a kettle.

"How did you find me here?" She pulled out mugs and the instant coffee. It stored better for longer. It would also hide any bitter taste if she added poison. She had some because a woman living alone in the woods invested in many kinds of protection.

If she killed him, she'd have to dispose of the body. The compost heap out back came to mind. What if people came looking, though? His family didn't seem the type to just let him disappear.

"I got your address from a guy."

"You exposed me to a stranger?" she hissed, turning around and slamming the cups on the counter.

"No. 'Course not." He stood in her living room. Sunshine watched him, entirely too fascinated.

It made Lainey terse. "Liar. I know you exposed

me. Earlier, you said you bought information from the IRS."

Raymond frowned. "Okay, so the guy who sent me the info knows your name and stuff, but not why I wanted it."

Didn't matter. She'd have to ditch this identity. "You're an idiot. Never involve other people if you can avoid it."

"I wouldn't have had to if you'd not acted so mysterious."

"It's called being discreet." She rolled her eyes. "And to think your dumb ass bypassed my security."

"Um, what security?" He looked baffled, which was when Sunshine giggled.

"I did dat."

"What?" They both looked at the little girl spinning and kicking her feet.

Lainey's gaze narrowed. "What do you mean, you did it? Did you mess with the security system?"

Sunshine nodded. "I pressed lots of buttons."

Don't yell. Don't yell. Lainey had been raised with lots of yelling, and it had rubbed off. "What the hell, Sunshine? Why would you do that?"

"So Daddy could surprise you."

10

Lainey almost fell over. "Excuse me? What did you just say?"

"Dat my daddy. Like in the picture." Her child made the pronouncement, smiling the entire time, and poor Raymond appeared as if he might just die of a heart attack.

He had definitely stopped breathing.

"Don't listen to her. You're not her father." Sunshine's daddy didn't actually exist. According to the doctors who made her, Lainey got a cocktail fertilizing her egg.

"Yes, he is."

"No, he's not," Lainey snapped as she pulled out a bottle of booze. She was pretty sure Raymond could use a slug of brandy. She certainly could. Each mug got a dollop. Despite Sunshine's attempt to kill them by shock, she added marshmallows to her mug of hot cocoa mix then came around the counter to snare Sunshine and perch her on a stool.

"You live here alone?" he asked, nearing the kitchen island.

"Are you fishing for information?"

"Just making conversation."

"I can't believe you just showed up," she muttered. "Ever think of calling ahead?"

"And give you warning?" Again, he flashed that damnable grin.

"Which goes to show your visit is unwelcome."

Sunshine took that moment to protest. "You no want my daddy to visit?"

That put an end to their bickering as they both stared at Sunshine.

As if synchronized they both spoke.

"I'm not—"

"He's not—"

"—*your daddy.*"

Sunshine's lower lip wobbled. Tears trembled in her eyes. But she didn't give in to them. Just said the saddest, softest, "Okay."

Lainey wondered if Raymond felt as big of an asshole as she did. Still, she'd never lied to Sunshine before and wasn't about to start now.

The kettle whistled, and she poured out the hot water. "Who knows you're here?" She didn't worry about Raymond too much. He wasn't a fighter, not like some of his siblings. Even if he did try and attack, she had a block of knives behind her and a Glock hidden in the second drawer of the island.

"No one knows."

"Bull," she said, biting off the shit part.

"I'm not stupid. Given the lengths you went to hide, I had a feeling you wouldn't want that knowledge broadcast."

"Says the guy who poked his nose in after being told to leave things alone." She glared at him.

Sunshine didn't like it. "No be mad, Mommy."

"Yeah, Mommy," he teased.

Did the man want to die?

"Hungry." Her little girl stated and rubbed her belly. "You hungry?" Her child beamed at Raymond, wisps of hair curling around her perfect face. Her hair was a platinum that bordered on white.

"Uh, sure. I could eat."

"Steak!" Sunshine clapped her hands.

Lainey mentally revised what she had thawed. "I only have venison."

"That's fine."

She glanced at Raymond. He didn't appear to be leaving anytime soon. "It'll be about half an hour. Why don't you get changed, baby girl, while I get it ready?"

"M'kay." Sunshine bolted for the stairs, fat braid bouncing behind her.

He watched her go then turned to Lainey. "Is she like us? Made in a lab?"

"I already told you we're nothing alike."

"We were both created," he stated.

She wanted to sigh in annoyance because lying at this point served no purpose. She opened the fridge to pull out packages of meat and some fixings to make him a side dish.

"Well?" he prodded.

"Yes, I was made in a lab. Not the same one as you. They had me shaken and stirred in the European branch."

"There are more labs?" A dumb reply, then again, how would he know? The knowledge of them was kept from the common folk.

"Not anymore," was her smug reply as she seasoned the meat.

"You destroyed them? Alone?" He sounded surprised.

"Is it because I'm a girl you're having a hard time believing it?" she asked, pivoting to her stove and firing up the flames under the indoor grill. She turned on the fan. She'd learned her lesson the first time she smoked the kitchen.

"I'm simply impressed is all. I'm having the shittiest time trying to find out anything and you managed to take down not just one lab, but many."

"Don't feel too bad. They had the best hiding them." She would know. She used to be a part of that security.

He frowned. "You said before that we were lucky because we got out young. How old were you when you escaped?"

"Old enough to know what they're capable of." She wouldn't allow her hands to tremble. She'd left the nightmare of her upbringing behind.

He glanced to the staircase. "Is she yours or…"

"Did I steal her?" Her query ended on a lilt. "Depends how you look at it. I'm sure Mr. X would claim Sunshine is his property, but that's my egg that made her. My body that incubated and birthed her. She's my daughter, and she belongs to no one."

"You had a baby." His eyes widened. "Meaning Anika should be okay."

"I had a baby and was okay. Anika's situation isn't mine. Which is why I referred you to John." Then a grudgingly added, "He was the one who helped me with Sunshine." Which galled because she would have preferred not to tell anyone about the life growing inside her. However, she'd known she needed help.

"But it is possible to have a healthy child."

"Yes."

"And is she…" Again, he trailed off.

She wanted to shake him. He'd tracked her down, and now he hesitated? "Does she take after me? Yes."

"And what are you, exactly?" He'd actually asked the one question she wasn't ready to answer.

"Take a guess."

"If I were to go by hair coloring, white tiger?"

She snickered. "Nope."

"Llama?" He wrinkled his nose.

That made her laugh. "Not even close. That's just a screen name."

"Are you feline?"

"Nope."

"Wolf?"

She shook her head.

"Bear? Fox?" He named an impressive array of possibilities, but she knew he'd never guess.

Trust Sunshine to spill the secret as she returned, crab walking upside down on the ceiling overhead before flipping to land on the counter, silvery hair streaming. "We're vampires!"

11

THE FACT SUNSHINE HAD PULLED A HORROR-movie trick along with the announcement she was a vampire had him gaping. Surely the child jested, but a glance at Lainey's face—the bleakness of her expression—had him whispering, "How is that possible?"

"Werewolves exist, why not vampires?" she quipped, and yet her tone held no mirth.

"Vampires." He whispered the word, trying to align his perception of them with the woman and child in front of him.

Sunshine, wearing pale blue overalls and a pink top, sat on the island and scooched to be nearer him. He eyed her for signs of a bloodthirsty monster.

She was an adorable little girl with normal teeth and a curious expression. She held out her arms.

Having had many young siblings, he knew how to grab her and perch her on the seat beside him. Then he glanced between mother and daughter.

"You don't look dead," he finally said.

Lainey snorted. "Because, for one, vampires are not actually dead. They just work differently biologically than most mammals. Two, we're not full-blooded vamps. I'm a splice, and Sunshine is a piece of that, plus whatever else they gave me." She seasoned the venison.

"Any other legends that are real?"

"I hear the djinn are real, too, but they haven't had luck trapping one yet."

"What else, the Loch Ness monster?"

"Now you're just being silly." She whirled with the steaks, slapping them into the hot pan with its sizzling glob of bacon grease. The microwave beeped, and the potatoes were ready.

It gave him time to compose himself, and being a bit of a geek, he had to ask. "I'm surprised you get electrical service this far outside the city."

"We don't. The house has solar roof tiles that keep a large bank of batteries charged. We also have a buried backup propane tank to run a generator and some appliances."

"You're off grid,"

"As much as I can be."

The steaks were flipped a minute after hitting the

pan. He almost drooled at the smell, but he forgot food as Lainey pulled out a bottle of red liquid. He didn't need to ask what she poured. He could smell it.

Blood.

Which the little girl grabbed and guzzled.

Don't freak out. He knew this was a test from the way Lainey took her time with her cup and eyed him over the rim. Her gaze dared him to ask.

So he did. "Is it human?"

"Yes."

"Where do you get it?"

"What you really want to know is, do I kill for it?" She paused, and he debated how far to the door before she added, "No one died to feed us."

Good to know. "How often do you need blood?"

"A few ounces daily to curb the craving, but given we're not full vampires, we can supplement our diet with other food."

"That's handy. Other than blood drinking, what other vampire traits do you have? Can you turn into a bat?"

"No." Looking quite put out, Sunshine pursed her lips. "Mavis can."

He didn't know who that was.

Lainey supplied the answer. "Vlad's daughter in the animated movie *Hotel Transylvania*."

"Oh."

"I can hide good," Sunshine interjected.

"Understatement. Sunshine can slip into shadows and use them as cover," Lainey explained. "We both can."

"That's cool." And he meant it. To him that made them superhero like. Even as his mind reminded him they drank human blood.

"I have to ask, why would Mr. X want a vampire mix?"

"Because of the mind control abilities." She stared straight at him and said, "Sleep."

12

Lainey did nothing as Raymond's eyes closed and gravity took over. His body slid to the floor.

Sunshine yelped. "Daddy fell."

"He's not your daddy," Lainey grumbled.

But Sunshine wasn't listening as she crouched beside Raymond and patted his cheek. "Wakey-wakey."

"He's not waking, sweetheart. At least not until after we're gone." Or so she hoped. She hadn't whammied anyone in a while. Nice to know she still could. It didn't work on everyone.

Her daughter's lower lip jutted. "No wanna go."

Crouching brought Lainey to her level. "We kind of have to, Sunshine. He found us. It's not safe."

"Okay. But Daddy come, too."

She gritted her teeth. "He can't come."

"Wanna keep him." Her daughter threw herself on him.

"You can't just keep him, baby girl. People aren't things you own."

"But he my daddy." Again with the certainty and the tugging down of the corners of her lips.

Lainey eyed Raymond. She wanted to argue and say it was impossible. They didn't belong to the same lab. He'd been three when he left, making it unlikely they'd harvested sperm. Even if they had later grabbed some from him, once they rediscovered his existence, she just couldn't see Mr. X wasting in vitro fertilization using the sperm of what he thought was a dud subject.

Given Sunshine had more vampire traits than Lainey, she suspected the father was most likely a blood drinker, too.

Sunshine was Lainey two point oh. While she got some of the basic stuff like simple mind control—enough to suggest to someone open to listening, like poor Raymond—her daughter was proving to be not only stronger in that aspect but also very intelligent. Which might be a hereditary thing rather than a specific vampire trait.

Originally, the Xlabs were interested in Lainey's rapid healing abilities, which made her almost impervious to all damage. Harnessing it would have been a boon to the pharmaceutical industry if not for two things. One, most subjects didn't fare well for long periods in the sun, and two, most humans injected with vampire genetics eventually turned into monsters.

Lainey excluded. But at times, when her daughter had a moment where she regressed and had a tantrum, she wondered if she'd end up losing her to the bloodthirsty monster inside. She had to hope that as Sunshine got older, she'd better control her urges.

Leaning down beside Sunshine, she asked, "Why do you think he's your daddy? Did you have a dream?" Lainey didn't have any precognition ability, but Sunshine did, and Lainey knew better than to ignore it.

"You'll see." Sunshine patted his unconscious cheek. "He wuvs me. He protects me when the bad man comes."

The words froze Lainey. Through stiff lips, she managed to ask, "What bad man?"

"Don't worry, Mommy. He only comes when there's snow on the ground."

Not exactly reassuring, given that could happen any day now. Luckily, the last forecast hadn't shown anything for the next few days. She had room to breathe and plan. Pack. Decide how to deal with Raymond.

Out of curiosity, she eyed Sunshine. "What should we do?"

"Daddy has a plan."

"*Daddy* didn't know you existed ten minutes ago. I highly doubt he's got a plan to save us."

"Silly Mommy. Daddy will fix it." With a giggle, Sunshine rose. "I go for walk? It's dark."

Lainey almost said no. With mention of the bad man coming, she wanted to lock up her daughter, flee, do anything but deal with the idea someone might hurt Sunshine or try and take her away.

But Lainey wasn't a coward or prone to panic. Not to mention she'd been teaching Sunshine to be self-sufficient, planning for a day when she might not be around. Her daughter could handle herself better than most. Besides, with Sunshine out of hearing on her daily run in the fresh air around the cabin, she could deal with Raymond.

Apply pressure and deprive him of blood and oxygen to the brain would result in a quick, painless death. Also a waste when a slice to the carotid artery would harvest a fresh supply of blood for their trip. She hadn't killed for the blood in her fridge, but she had and would if it proved necessary to feed them.

He'd give them more than enough to travel for a few days.

However, if he died, Sunshine would be pissed. She seemed awfully interested in Raymond Hubbard, but that wasn't the only reason Lainey allowed him to live. Her conscience nagged. He hadn't done anything to hurt her other than show up. In his place, she would have probably done the same.

What to do then? She stared down at his face, handsome in forced sleep. The smell of him made her gums ache. A longing filled her. To touch his cheek. Brush back his hair. Pretend for a second she was that happy stick lady in the picture, holding hands, big smiles under a full moon. Like a real family.

The longing filled her with the hope of possibility. But rather than give in to it, she walked away.

13

RAYMOND WOKE FEELING WELL RESTED, HIS head on a pillow, a blanket smelling of the outdoors as if dried on a clothesline pulled over him. However, the bed he lay on could have used some cushion. Then again, what could he expect from sleeping on the floor?

How did he get there? Last he recalled he was chatting with Lainey and Sunshine about their vampire powers while drinking his coffee

She drugged me!

But obviously not for carnal delights. He remained clothed.

Pushing upright, he caught the murmur of voices. He glanced over to see Sunshine, the precious little girl who desperately wanted a daddy, sitting in front of a computer screen, Lainey leaning over her, pointing.

Online learning, he surmised, having had to deal with it when his siblings had to stay home during the pandemic. It made sense. Sunshine couldn't exactly go to a normal school. He pushed to his feet, and Lainey murmured to Sunshine before heading over.

"What did you do to me?" he asked, rubbing the knot on the side of his head.

"Put you to sleep for a bit so I could figure out the best thing for Sunshine and me."

"You drugged my coffee."

"Nope. More like a mental suggestion."

He blinked as he recalled her last words. Something about mind control. "That's kind of disturbing you can do that."

"Not my fault you were so receptive to it."

"Wasn't expecting it," he muttered. He'd be more on guard for next time. On guard for what, he couldn't say. He had no idea how it happened or how to stop it.

"Are you going to whine about the fact I took you down or ask what the plan is?"

"Given you didn't kill or abandon me, I assume I'm a part of it."

Her lips pursed. "Sunshine insists we need you."

Which obviously didn't sit well with Mama. "We'll be leaving at sunset."

"Why not now?"

"Too close to dawn. Vampire. Remember? She doesn't do daylight well. Why do you think we live here?"

"I thought Alaska had almost twenty-four-hour sun in the summer."

"It does, which is when we visit an old friend with a spare bedroom."

His eyes widened. "John."

"Even if she only gets about six hours of full darkness during Ontario's peak, it's better than nothing. While John minds her, I can get lots of shopping done."

"This world is getting smaller and smaller," he observed.

"Or bigger depending on how you look at it."

An interesting perspective given how much he'd learned of late. "So what is the plan? We leave here at sunset and go where?"

"Nunavut."

"Isn't that even more remote?"

"Yes. If you don't like it, you don't have to go."

"Oh, I'm coming." He wasn't about to leave, and not just because he needed answers. When he'd embarked on this trip to find PinkLlama, he'd been angry and curious, also plenty fearful. What he didn't expect was to become even more curious, but he traded the anger for intrigue and the fear for something that oddly felt like protectiveness.

In Lainey, he could see someone on edge, stressing like he had been, feeling alone and burdened. He wanted to ease that strain.

"Once we leave, we don't stop until we're over the border. That means no pee breaks, so bring a cup."

"What about gas?"

"My tank is full, plus there's another fifty gallons strapped to the roof. We shouldn't need to stop."

"I'm going to guess that letting my family know I'm okay is a no-no?"

She arched a brow. "What do you think?

"I won't be able to remain incommunicado forever."

"Until we're safely away and can acquire a secure means of contact, you'll have to do without your family."

"You drive a tough bargain."

"If you don't like it, leave."

He shook his head. "You know I can't."

"Because you want answers."

He did, but it was more than that. The woman in front of him intrigued him. Made him see her in a way he saw few people. And she appeared to see him right back. The moment between them stretched, fraught with tension.

Possibility.

Sunshine took that moment to holler, "This is stupid."

That made Lainey sigh. "I knew she'd do this. She'd rather be talking to you than doing her schoolwork."

"How about I help her? I do it for my siblings all the time."

Biting her lower lip, Lainey hesitated for a second before nodding. "Fine. But watch yourself. She's good at ferreting secrets."

Like he'd be fooled by a child.

At first, Sunshine didn't try. He sat beside her on a stool and explained the problem on her screen. At her age, she should be learning numbers and letters. What he saw was fractions that required multiplication and division.

And she caught on to the math quick once he explained it. Watching her work, Raymond was reminded of himself. The kid was bright. She understood with little explanation. She was also sly. Before he knew it, he'd inadvertently spilled his first secret.

"You're good at dis," lisped the girl.

"I had practice."

"You has brothers and sisters?"

"Mostly I helped my brothers. My sisters are smart."

Sunshine grinned. "Girls rule. Mommy said so."

"Yes, they do." His turn for a question. "Do you ever go to the town?"

Sunshine shook her head. "When mommy has to go, I hides in my special room."

"What's your special room?"

Lainey heard and answered. "Think of a panic room built to withstand detection and attack." Lainey clapped her hands. "That's enough, little missy. Time for you to get ready for bed. We have a big adventure happening when you get up."

"Tuck me in." She turned the biggest eyes on Raymond, and he couldn't say no. It involved many of the rituals he remembered with Maeve and Daeve then, later on, Daphne. His younger brother Tyson had been more independent—and haunted—than the rest.

Raymond brushed his teeth with her, counting the strokes with his borrowed toothbrush. He dragged a comb through her hair. One hundred strokes that she counted in French. His hands weren't as deft as Stefan's, who could weave a French braid, but he could manage a simple fat version.

Then he read a chapter from *Anne of Green Gables*, the oddest story for a vampire girl her age. Then again, what did he know? A day ago, he hadn't even known her kind existed.

By the time he was done, he could tell dawn must have arrived. The body just knew Instinctively. He slid out of the bedroom with its spinning orb light that cast unicorns and stars on the ceiling. Heading downstairs, he found Lainey in the kitchen, rinsing the dishes. An odd thing to worry about given they'd be leaving later that day.

It was also the first time they had been alone. Why it should suddenly matter, he couldn't quite decipher, and yet he was very aware of her as a woman.

"Can I help you clean up?"

She didn't turn around, but her entire posture stiffened. "I'm fine." Then a grudging, "Thanks."

"Your kid is pretty awesome."

"I know."

"I am really sorry I fucked shit up for you guys."

She turned and rolled her shoulders. "It was bound to happen eventually."

"Have you had to move before?"

"When she was young, I never stayed in one place too long. But that's no way to raise a kid."

"Looks like you've been here a while."

"Three years. Which was probably one year too many. And I knew it. I just wanted to try and give

Sunshine a bit longer before I took her from the only home she knows."

"Why are you so worried still? The labs are gone." Yet like him, she remained ill at ease. He could have predicted her answer.

"Mr. X is still out there."

It made him wonder. "Is that who Sunshine means when she says the bad man is coming?"

"Maybe." Lainey shrugged.

"Has Sunshine ever been wrong with a prediction?"

"No." The short replies only served to highlight her agitation. Her hands were fists by her sides.

He didn't need the course he'd taken on human behavior to realize she stood on a tightrope emotionally. Raymond wasn't good with offering the kind of comfort people needed. He fixed things in other ways. But he found himself moving to her and grabbing her hands. Squeezing them and saying, "It will be okay."

She glanced at him, and he noticed a tremor in her lips. "You can't be sure of that."

"No, but I can promise to do my best to protect you."

"I don't need your protection," she said harshly, and yet she didn't pull out of his grip.

"Then let me be your friend." He wanted nothing

more in that moment than to offer her his support. To take the strain out of her bearing.

"I can't…" She trailed off.

Couldn't let him close. Didn't dare. But even as he read that in her words and expression, he saw the longing, the need that she couldn't express aloud.

How was it he felt her emotions? Wanted to fix her turmoil?

He used a finger to tilt her chin upward. "I'm not leaving you."

"You don't even know me."

"So what?" It didn't matter they'd just met. For the first time in a long time, Raymond felt something for someone.

When his mom had told him how she'd known within an hour that her husband, a man who died before their arrival, would be the love of her life, he'd scoffed. Not anymore. He suddenly understood what she'd meant about feeling a connection to someone so strong that it overrode everything else.

Blame his social awkwardness for speaking his mind. "I want to kiss you."

Rather than reply, or slap him, she pressed her mouth to his.

14

WHY AM I KISSING HIM?

The very fact took her by surprise. He'd asked. She could have said no. Could have moved away or done any number of things.

But instead, she'd pressed her lips to his, her first kiss in a long time. Living in the shadows meant forgoing the opportunities others had to make connections.

It wasn't that she didn't want any. She just had a lack of time and too many secrets. When she did her yearly solstice visit to John's place, she went out and, yes, satisfied that need to be touched by someone. But it always lacked something.

Pleasures of the flesh didn't always translate to the mind. She was always wound so tight, fearful of giving something away. Of shocking.

Raymond knew her secret. It didn't scare him. He didn't shy away. He was right. He was like her. While she denied it, in many ways they were the same.

She didn't have to hide from him. It elevated the kiss from something simple to her holding his head that she might plunder his mouth.

If he'd been surprised and hesitant at first, he lost it quickly. He grabbed her around the waist and gripped her tight. His tongue danced with hers.

She shimmied back until her ass hit the counter. As if he read her mind, he lifted her and sat her on it then stripped off her pants.

It was madness. It was necessary. They had no time. Once the sun set, they'd be on the run. Looking over their shoulders. Wiping their traces with a child in tow.

She would take a moment of pleasure right now. Now before she ditched him during their flight and disappeared.

Her hands skimmed the shirt from his torso, and she raked her nails down his chest. He hissed, in pleasure, not pain. Her cheeks rested on the counter, her panties' thin cotton not hiding the chill of the wooden top. Her shirt was tossed aside, and she didn't wear a bra. Why would she at home?

He groaned. No words, just worship with his mouth as he latched onto a nipple and sucked. How he sucked and teased. And pleased.

She tugged at his pants and shoved at them, eager to feel him inside, only he dropped to his knees. She would have screamed if he'd not parted her legs enough he could press his mouth against her.

Oh. She knew she had to keep her noises low. She didn't want to wake her kid, but dammit, it felt so good to have him nuzzling her then shoving the fabric aside that he could lick her.

She clutched his head with one hand and braced back on the other as she let her hips roll and ride against his mouth. She came, sharp and quick, but he didn't relent. He flicked her clit and drove his fingers into her until she panted and tightened anew. Only then did he slip into her. The thick length of him filling her. She clutched both his shoulders as he held her by the ass, using his grip to drive her onto his shaft. Pulling and grinding, shoving into her deep enough he kept rubbing that inner sweet spot, and when she came this time, it was biting at his neck, trying to mask the satisfied, guttural growl trembling in her.

With a harsh gasp, he pulled from her, and she felt the hot wetness as he came against her thigh.

At least one of them had the forethought to pull out.

It also served as a wakeup reminder that, while pleasurable, they still had much preparing to do.

She shoved at him and hopped off the counter. "There's a shower if you need one. I gotta check the fluids on the truck." Being outside gave her a chance to take a few deep breaths and then castigate herself.

What had she done? And why was she craving more already?

15

Lainey paced inside the garage rather than opening the hood of the truck.

What had she done? Bad enough she kissed the man, but she just had to go and screw him. And screw him good.

She could even now be pregnant. She wasn't dumb. Lainey knew that pulling out wasn't one hundred percent effective. Precum? A very real thing.

The only reassuring thing was the reminder of her fertility issues. Despite being a prisoner, because of good behavior she'd received some privileges the others didn't. Like having sex with the guards, nurses, technicians. She'd had nothing better to do, and a part of her always hoped one of them would have the balls to help her escape.

They didn't.

And back then, she couldn't whammy people because of the contact lenses they made her wear.

Talk about restrictive having to stare at people in the eye to mesmerize them.

She had no shortage of people who wanted to sleep with her. Man. Woman. The doctors encouraged it. Hoped she'd get pregnant the old-fashioned way. From the moment she began ovulating at fourteen, they began harvesting her eggs. But her eggs apparently didn't like being outside her body. So, they left them inside her and attempted artificial insemination, which failed so many times she stopped counting.

"Why can't she get pregnant?" was the question she heard all the time. The replies weren't kind.

It discouraged to be reminded of how defective they considered her while, at the same time, prizing her. She was a shining example of how a vampire mix could work. Now if only they could stop the others from going mad. In her late twenties, Lainey held the record for longevity. The others with the same kind of mix, after a certain amount of time, regressed into a vicious state.

She'd seen it once. It was ugly, violent and bloody. Please don't ever let her become a monster. And what of her daughter? Could Lainey help her retain her sense of humanity?

As she paced the garage, she took note of the

things she had inside. Not much. Her truck. A lawn-mower. Weed trimmer. A few other tools. Gas cans to power the machines, an old snowmobile, and an ATV.

She'd have to leave almost all of it behind and start over. She didn't have a choice. This was about more than just her possibly of being recaptured. She couldn't let Mr. X get his hands on Sunshine, a child who shouldn't exist. The fact that those mixed with vampire genetics had been thought unable to impregnate or carry to term made Sunshine an even bigger miracle.

If the bad man was coming, he'd better be ready to fight because Lainey would do anything to keep her safe.

That thought made her grab a pair of gas cans. She took them outside and made a circuit around the house, even splashing some on the siding. The loop finished with her by the front door. It opened, and Raymond stood in the opening.

The sun shone bright. "Close it."

He stepped outside in his socks and no coat, the air's sharp bite making her shiver inside her sweater.

"What are you doing?" he asked.

She set the gas cans down. "Preparing to wipe our presence."

He arched a brow. "Seems pretty permanent. Don't you want to come back?"

She didn't want to leave. She had no choice. "It's just a place. We'll make a new home."

"I'm—"

She cut him off. "If you say sorry one more time, I will hit you."

His mouth snapped shut. Then because he just couldn't help himself, "Thank you."

"For what?" she asked, confused. For threatening bodily harm?

"For, you know." He shifted with discomfort. "Thank you for what we did. Earlier. In the kitchen."

Fuck me he was blushing because he'd brought up the most awkward moment possible, the thing she'd finally managed to push aside. His words brought it all back. Heat flushed her cheeks—and other parts. "It was nothing.

"Not to me."

By the expression on his face he might not have meant to admit that. Lainey's common sense didn't render her immune to flattery. She almost smiled in pleasure, only to remind herself not to get close. "I'm not looking for a boyfriend." A rebuke that brought disappointment to his expression.

"I get it."

"Do you? I'm not a simple girl you can just date."

"Never asked you to be simple. I like you're complex, or I wouldn't be acting like such a dork."

He rubbed his face. "Forgive me. I don't get out of my basement often."

The crushing honesty reminded her she'd not been around many people either. Trust didn't come easily. She changed the subject. "You drove here in a car?"

"It's a rental."

"It's useless if we get any snow."

"Good thing I'm going with you."

She chewed her lower lip. It hadn't occurred to her they'd travel in the same vehicle. She'd assumed he'd follow.

He then said softly, "I know you want to ditch me, but I can help."

"I don't need you."

"I know you don't. Think of it more as helping my family. Mr. X is as much a danger to us as you. Helping you helps us. As allies we can be stronger together."

It would be nice to not fight alone. "Fine. You can come in the truck. But if you do anything to jeopardize..." She wagged a finger as she came up the steps until she drew eye level with him.

"I'll be good. I swear." He couldn't hold her gaze; it ducked shyly then glanced past her. A frown formed. "I see dark clouds on the horizon."

"What?" She whirled. "Those are not supposed to be there." She'd checked the forecast earlier, and according to it, they had a few more days before they were supposed to expect any precipitation.

The phone appeared in Raymond's hand as if by magic. He was already searching as he entered the house with her on his heels. "Looks like something shifted in the weather patterns. A storm has developed and is tracking to arrive around four in the afternoon."

And it was two o'clock already. Sunshine's warning rang in her ears. The bad man would come with the snow.

"Shit." She glanced upstairs. A stream of profanity left her lips. "Fucking shit. Hell. Damn."

Raymond shoved his phone in his pocket as he approached her, concern in his gaze. When he would have reached out, she shied away and paced. "We need to leave now."

"Good thing we're packed."

"The truck isn't," she grumbled. She'd not even pulled out of the garage yet. "I'm going to get it." She snared the keys, and as she headed outside, the bright sun hit her as if in stark mockery to the dark clouds approaching.

"Want me to wake the kid?" he called from the door.

"Not yet. I want to load the truck first." She eyed the distance to the garage, which the previous owner for some reason had placed several car lengths away.

Times like this, she wished she'd had a covered walkway built from the house to the garage. "I don't want her outside while it's this bright. Preferably we'll get some cloud cover, and even then, she will have to be swaddled." Sunshine's skin did not react well to UV light. Lainey could tolerate it, although she wasn't crazy about bright, sunny days, and she never went uncovered to a beach.

"I assume your vehicle has blacked-out windows?"

"Sunshine can travel in it safely. I'll move it to the front door. You start bringing out the gear." She pointed to the pile assembled. Bug-out bags, which were always ready to go, but also others of the treasures they'd accumulated together. It might make the move easier on Sunshine if she got to keep some of her things. Lainey also included food and drink in coolers. Getting meat and blood on the run might be difficult.

The big garage held more than just her truck. It also had a snowmobile and a four-wheeler. But Sunshine couldn't travel with those during the day. Lainey had long hoped Sunshine might grow out of her allergy, but it got worse as she aged, going from able to tolerate with red skin to blistering and bubbling. A good thing she healed fast.

It had been a full two years since her last actual exposure, and it had been bad. Sunshine had decided she wanted to go outside despite it still being daylight. She waited until Lainey was in the bathroom. Mid pee, Lainey heard the screams and stood. She'd pissed all over the floor and herself in her panic to help her child. Rushing out, Lainey found her daughter sobbing just inside the front door, scorched and in pain.

She never did it again.

Lainey parked her pickup truck in front of the house, the bed covered by a cap that had no windows. While she hated putting Sunshine in it, out of sight, it proved the most discreet and comfortable way for her child to travel. People also didn't remark on it like they did the blacked-out SUV with the custom barrier behind the back seat. It took only one muttered, "Pedovan," and she'd swapped it for the truck.

As Raymond emerged from the house, hands full, the first cold snowflake hit her cheek and melted. The sunshine only served to highlight the darkness of the approaching bank of clouds, a roiling mass that had her stomach tightening in fear.

"We have to go. Now!" She left him to pack as she raced into the house for her daughter. As she hit the bottom step, Sunshine appeared, already dressed. Long-sleeve shirt tucked inside gloves. A facemask with thinner fabric for the eyes, slid into the neckline. Her pants were tucked into socks.

Lainey wanted to cry to see her calmly accepting and ready. But she had to be strong.

She grabbed the last of Sunshine's outfit, jacket with hood, sunglasses, and boots. When done, Sunshine was a marshmallow of layers, clutching her favorite stuffed toy, a gray and silver lynx.

As Raymond walked in, the sudden connection hit her like a slap. Having learned all kinds of things about Raymond, including his shifting animal, Lainey wondered just how long her daughter had known he'd be entering their lives. Because she highly doubted the favorite toy came about by coincidence.

"That storm is moving in crazy fast," he remarked, a dusting of snow melting as he stepped in and quickly closed the door.

"We're ready to go." Lainey's claim drew his gaze to the swaddled Sunshine.

"Looking good, Marshmallow Princess. Shall we go for a ride?" He held out his arms, and Lainey's daughter had no hesitation throwing herself at him.

Funny how they both completely trusted this man and felt drawn to him. Having him around showed what it would be liked to perhaps have a partner to share the burden. It was nice. She just couldn't see it ending well.

The snow began to fall faster. More and more flakes swirled, heightening her tension.

Bad man is coming with the snow.

They had to leave. Now. Sunshine was tucked in the back, her expression hidden behind a mask. The fear must have been overwhelming.

Lainey wanted to succumb, but she had to be strong.

She grabbed the hatch to close it, but Raymond stopped her. For a second, she thought he would climb in with Sunshine.

"Hey, princess, do you need some company?"

Tears pricked Lainey's eyes. Stupid and yet she couldn't help herself at the kindness. She lost a drop when Sunshine replied with, "I think you should ride with Mommy. She needs you."

Another premonition, or her daughter playing matchmaker with a man she wanted to call Daddy?

Didn't matter. She'd prefer to have another set of eyes up front. The hatch closed with her murmuring, "Love you, baby girl."

"Wuv you more."

She took a deep breath then another as she gave her house a last look. A cute cabin that had survived decades until her arrival.

Sorry, house. You were good to us, but we can't let them get their hands on anything. Even a strand of hair left behind could pose a danger.

Lainey knelt and lit her butane lighter. She touched the flickering flame to the gas she'd poured.

The ring of fire zipped around the house and up the wooden beams in the spots she'd splashed it. As she got in the truck, she made a point of ignoring her mirrors, knowing she'd burned any hope of ever coming back.

The engine roared as she hit the gas pedal. The disadvantage to living remotely was the lack of roads in the area. Usually she would have relied on her security system to be her eyes and guide to avoid possible threats, but given she'd yet to get it functioning again properly since Sunshine played with it, she was moving blind.

And she meant that quite literally.

The visibility on the road turned to shit and quick. The sun disappeared as she raced toward the stormy horizon. No choice. She had to follow the road. The falling snow led to the barely two-lane tarmac that had already accumulated a few inches. She engaged the four-wheel drive and ignored the side roads, most going deeper into the remote areas of Alaska.

The highway she needed was closer to the city. Not that she planned on driving to Nunavut in this weather. They'd have to wait out the storm.

"We should have left earlier," she muttered, clutching the steering wheel in a death grip. She should have loaded the truck and left the moment Sunshine predicted danger.

"I doubt it would have mattered. If your daughter sees the future, and it always comes to pass, then that would suggest that there is an inevitability when it comes to preset events."

She slewed a scowl in his direction. "Fuck you. I have free will."

"You do. Seeing the future doesn't change that. The future takes into account the fact you will act. At the same time, those actions always lead to the predicted outcome."

"That's kind of pessimistic."

"If premonitions don't come true because they influence a person to change events, then they are not premonitions."

Clutching the wheel, she tried to see past the falling snow. "I can't believe you're arguing semantics with me right now."

"Would you prefer to argue about something different?" he asked. "We could talk about what happened this morning."

"Nothing to talk about."

"Usually I would agree and be happy that you wanted to avoid it. Trust me, I'm not a guy who likes attachment or messy emotional outbursts, but…" He trailed off.

She couldn't help herself. "But what?"

"This is going to sound corny, but there's something between us."

It did sound corny, yet at the same time true. Still, she wasn't about to sound just as dorky and admit it. "It was just sex."

"Not for me it wasn't. It was incredible. You're incredible."

There he went flattering her again.

"You're wasting your breath. That was the one and only time we'll ever sleep together."

"Is this where I point out we've never slept?"

"Don't you play word games with me," she huffed, and yet she enjoyed herself.

"Don't lie then."

"When did I lie?"

"We both know it's going to happen again. And again."

She gripped the wheel. His cockiness knew no bounds. His arrogance annoyed, mostly because it was true. If the chance arose, she would indulge again.

She said nothing. Eventually, he did. "Do you know this is the farthest I've ever gone from home?"

"Seriously?"

"Unless you count the lab I was taken from. But I don't remember that trip."

"How come you never leave the house?"

"I leave the house," was his defensive reply.

That made her snort. "I was watching you before

you showed up at my door. No, you don't. Not unless you have to and never for long."

He shrugged. "I am not a people person."

"You have no problem peopling with me." It sounded stupid the moment she said it, and he laughed.

"Because you're easy to talk to. You understand me. Even more than my family does. We've always been outsiders."

"I didn't want to be one. You seemed to have become one by choice."

"Be honest. You don't like being around lots of people."

She was about to deny it—to claim it was circumstance—only to pause. She'd hidden in big cities in the beginning, and the anonymity was easy. Only she couldn't help but feel out of place. The constant flow of strangers in her life was a source of anxiety. "Fine, I don't like crowds."

Before he could reply, she caught only the barest hint of something ahead. A moose charged across the road. She slammed on the brakes, and the truck spun out of control!

16

THE TRUCK SWERVED TO AVOID IMPACT. A good plan given the size of the damned moose. However, the maneuver and the braking on slick asphalt sent them spinning out of control. Fucking terrifying.

Raymond did his best to brace, fingers gripping the oh-shit bar, legs already apart, feet flexed for impact. The rapidness whiplashed his head, and he knew he'd feel it in his neck the next day. If there was a next day.

The car shifted on the road, the tires slipping from pavement to the snow-covered gravel just before the embankment. In dry conditions, they probably would have easily dipped in and out of the slight ditch, but the snow and ice made a mockery of the four-by-four. The truck tilted, and for a second, they wobbled, giving him hope they'd slam back down.

They weren't that lucky.

The laws of physics—with a helping hand from Murphy's Law—made the truck their bitch. It tilted on to its side. The impact squished him against his door while Lainey dangled in her seatbelt beside him.

"You okay?" Raymond managed.

"Fuck. Yes. No. Goddammit, I have to check on Sunshine." Lainey struggled to unbuckle and, when the clip released, landed on him heavily.

He absorbed the impact and thought she'd be happy she didn't splatter. For some reason, she went into a panic, thrashing and pushing. "I need out."

The confines of the truck obviously triggered her anxiety. He could understand that, even commiserate.

Until she nailed him in the balls.

A usually calm guy, the pain had Raymond snapping, "Calm the fuck down. She's probably fine. Better than me!"

Rather than reply, she yelled, "I'm coming, baby girl."

The only thing she heard was the whistle of the wind.

Surely Sunshine was fine. They hadn't rolled. She'd probably just gotten knocked around.

Oh no. Was she unconscious?

Great. Now he worried, too.

"Would you stop being a lump and help me? I need to check on her." Lainey shoved against him as she strained to open her truck door. From this angle it was heavy, especially with the wind trying to shove it closed and whipping inside.

Fuck that was cold. He couldn't stand beside her, not enough room, but he could give her a boost with his hands on her ass. The door heaved open, and she exited in a blast of swirling snow and ice.

The truck door slammed shut.

Raymond became very aware he was alone. He couldn't hear a thing beyond the storm and the engine still rumbling. He managed to catch a faint, "Sunshine!"

She shouldn't be out there in the storm alone.

He was already twisted partially out of his harness, so he clicked the button to release it and then stood. He was tall enough to shove open the driver's side door and get a face full of snow and ice. Pulling himself out, he was hit in the face by the whipping snow, making visibility poor despite the one working headlight.

Lainey's words carried on the biting cold. "Baby girl, you okay? Talk to me."

"I'm okay," Sunshine's higher-pitched voice reassured.

Raymond's tension didn't ease though. Sure, everyone had emerged unharmed, but their current mode of transportation appeared fucked. The truck rested on its side, motor still running, not that it did them any good with no tires on the ground. Four-by-four couldn't help here. They needed a winch at the very least.

In other words, they weren't getting out of here easily.

Raymond made his way to the back of the truck and found Lainey talking to her daughter as she cleared the snow that prevented her from opening the window.

As he neared, he shouted, "Hey, Marshmallow Princess, you okay in there?"

"I good," was the girl's reply. "It's cold."

He agreed and feared it would be getting colder. How he wished he'd dressed better as his lined lumber jacket did little to shield him from the brunt. "We'll see what we can do about that. Tuck in under those blankets for a minute while I help your mom dig out the door."

"Okay."

He dropped down and watched her frantically scooping to whisper, "We have a problem."

"No shit," Lainey muttered. "We're miles from anywhere with no means of getting around."

"I take it a tow truck isn't an option?"

"Storm like this, they'll stick close to the city rather than risk getting stuck out here." Lainey grimaced. "I don't suppose you have super lynx strength and can put us back on four wheels?"

He snorted. "I thought that was a vampire thing."

"I wish. All I got was an ability to heal quick, a dislike of daylight, and a penchant for blood." Lainey sighed. "I guess we're walking."

"In this storm? Don't be crazy. We'll hunker down until it's over."

"Where?"

"If we all huddle together in the truck with the extra clothes and stuff you brought, we can keep warm. We'll shut off the engine to save gas and run it only when we get too cold."

Her expression said quite clearly she wasn't crazy about his plan, and yet she didn't have many choices. She nodded. "It's probably best we ride out the storm rather than get lost in it. Help me get Sunshine out." She tugged to open the rear blacked-out window on the box to no avail. It would never open because of the angle.

"Hey, Sunshine, move away from the door and tuck your face against your knees."

No reply.

"Did you do it?"

A muffled, "Yes."

Lainey eyed him. "What are you doing?"

"Getting her out," he said before lifting a boot and snapping the Plexiglas.

At the first crack, Lainey threw herself at the jagged pieces and pulled. In moments she had her daughter. Hugging her so tight he had to fight not to join in.

He wanted to hug them both.

Lainey stood with the kid in her arms. "Let's get you into the cab. We're going to hunker here for a few hours."

"Camping!" Sunshine clapped her hands, thinking this was a grand adventure.

Lainey, however, appeared tense as they transferred all the blankets and clothes and some food to the cab. Only once it was stifling hot did they shut off the engine, which left them in the dark, sitting on a pile that started with clothing bags, then Raymond, then Lainey on Raymond's lap, then Sunshine curled up in hers, holding a stuffed lynx. She played a simple game on her tablet with a headset to hear it.

The toy had to be a coincidence. Surely the child couldn't truly predict the future.

"Can you stop thinking? It's driving me nuts."

He blinked. "I can't exactly stop."

"Go to sleep."

"I'm not tired." Understatement. He was wired for sound.

"I should go find help," she muttered.

"You mean go die? It will be hours of walking at the least, if you don't succumb to the storm."

"I'm tougher than I look."

"There's tough, and then there is taking an unnecessary chance. If anyone goes, it should be me."

"You'd die out there."

"It's a good thing I don't have a man card. I think you just shredded it." He'd caught the implication she didn't think him capable.

She shifted and turned in the glow of the tablet's screen, showing him a pensive face. "I didn't mean it as a dig on you. It's nasty out there."

"And you think you can handle it better than me?"

Lainey sagged against him. "No. But I feel so fucking useless just sitting here."

He understood the feeling. Surely they could do something.

What about talking about the real reason he'd hunted her down? "How much do you know about me?" Raymond asked.

"A lot." A coy reply.

"Anything in particular?"

She shifted in his lap in a way he didn't want to notice. And please, fucking god, don't let her notice that he'd noticed.

"Are we talking past or present? Because those are two very different things."

"You know about my past?"

"Not as much as I'd like. Your file was archived after your so-called death. It starts up again only a few years ago. And most of it turned out to be useless. You're smart and are online most of the time."

"Implying I never leave the house."

"Do you?"

"No, but I have good reasons."

"Name one."

"I have a hundred and thirty-one as of the crash. About to become one thirty-two."

"Let me guess, me."

"Actually, more like the awkward conversation. It wouldn't be happening if I'd stayed home."

"A lot of shit wouldn't have happened," she grumbled.

He became instantly contrite. "We'll fix this."

"Your optimism sucks. I blame your family."

"My family? What do they have to do with this?"

"You weren't careful. None of you. Living your best life in public."

"And obviously doing a good job given how long it took before anyone noticed." It killed that even he never figured any of it out before. If only his mother hadn't lied.

"It seems your run of dumb luck has ended."

"Mine or yours? You keep assuming this is my fault. Ever think maybe we shouldn't have run off into the storm? That maybe, just maybe, your kid was wrong about the danger coming?"

"We had to leave," Lainey stubbornly insisted.

"If we'd stayed, we'd still be safe and have options to escape."

Sunshine suddenly said loudly, "You would have died if we stayed." Sunshine's ominous words stopped the conversation.

The kid said nothing more. Neither did Lainey, as she kept turned from him, rigid and angry.

The only sound was the whistling of wind outside as the storm intensified. The situation was dire. He missed his hidey-hole at home more than anything, and yet, if given the choice, right that minute, he wouldn't have budged.

Despite the danger of their situation, he wanted to be here with Lainey and Sunshine.

"I'm sorry," he said. "I really, really hope we get out of here safely."

"And I'm sorry I snapped. I'm angry at myself right now because you're right. This is way worse than being snug in my house."

"Would it help if I said I've studied methods of living off the land and how to deal with inclement weather situations?" Knowledge helped with his anxiety about end-of-the-world scenarios.

"Reading isn't like doing."

"I've practiced."

"Where? In your basement?" she said with a snort.

And the discussion started. Raymond and Lainey talked in that darkness, him as much as her. Odd since he wasn't the chatty one of his family, and yet, he wanted to reassure them. So he regaled her with tales about his mom and siblings. Even told the embarrassing story of the first time he shifted because someone spiked a chocolate fountain with catnip at a backyard barbecue.

She told him sarcastic tales from her upbringing that gave him chills. Her laughter held a brittle edge, and he sensed she downplayed quite a bit of what happened. What he'd been spared.

No wonder she hated him.

About four hours into their crash, and the engine having just been shut off after warming the cab for the fourth time, Lainey fell asleep.

He thought Sunshine slumbered as well until she whispered, "Daddy?"

It never even occurred to him not to answer to that name. "What is it, princess?

"The bad man is close."

17

THEIR RESPITE WAS OVER. HE NUDGED Lainey awake. "We might have company."

"Fuck." She struggled for a moment before realizing they were packed in like a clown car. "I need to get out."

"We'll both get out."

Easier said than done. They first tucked Sunshine into the footwell, and then he boosted Lainey out.

"Remember, baby girl. If I say run, you bolt like a bunny in the forest and hide."

"Yes, Mommy."

Once Lainey left, it was Raymond's turn to go, but first he placed a hand on Sunshine's head. "Don't you worry, Marshmallow Princess. I won't let anyone hurt you."

"I know you won't, Daddy."

Raymond wasn't her father, he understood that, but in that moment, he wanted to be. He would act as a daddy, protecting his daughter against the enemy.

"Take dis." Sunshine handed him something that felt like a matchbook. He stuffed it into his pocket and, rather than ask why, said, "Thanks."

Emerging from the truck proved shockingly cold and nasty. The wind whipped snow, there was no visibility, and the wind terrified with its frigid tear, shaking tree limbs and whipping the snowscape.

A hand tapped him the moment he hit the ground. Lainey stood close to him, a good thing because he could barely see through the whipping snow. It was nine o'clock at night and pitch-black.

Lainey didn't shout. She didn't have to for him to hear. "Someone's coming."

He couldn't hear what drew her attention for another few seconds. Then he caught the steady rumble of an engine in the distance and, not long after, a refracting glow as if of light in the storm.

"I don't suppose it's a plow?" He was hopeful.

She dashed it. "This road is usually done last. Get behind the truck. If they're after me, they hopefully won't be expecting you."

"Or you hide, and I stay here so if it is bad news, they take one peek and keep on moving."

It wasn't the greatest plan, and yet she nodded. "Okay."

"Okay?" The acquiescence surprised.

"Sunshine said you'd have a plan."

"What? No— I—" Too late. Lainey left his side and he second-guessed his suggestion. He waited outside the truck and watched as the snow got brighter and the engine louder. When it finally emerged, he did what any normal stranded motorist would. He waved his arms. "Hey, you, broken down. A little bit of help?"

He hoped they stopped. For one, enemy or not, they had a working vehicle. A Good Samaritan wouldn't leave them stranded in a storm. A bad guy wouldn't get a choice in having his wheels taken from him once Raymond beat his ass.

The other vehicle stopped, the headlights pinning him with their brightness. He lifted an arm and moved to the side, trying to escape the bright glare. Four people dressed for the weather emerged from the truck. They left the engine running. As they neared, he did his best to look harmless. "Thanks for stopping. As you can see, I hit an icy patch. Could use a lift." He said nothing about the girls.

"Where are your passengers?" asked one of the strangers wearing a baclava and goggles. Not exactly travelling in vehicle attire.

"Don't know what you mean. It's just me out

here." He flashed what he hoped was a convincing smile.

"There's footsteps going around your vehicle." Another fellow, also wearing the head covering and eyewear, pointed.

Curse the bastard for having sharp eyes. "Oh. That's because, um…"

A gun emerged and pointed at Raymond's face. It should be noted this rarely ended up a positive thing in the movies or real life.

Raymond thought fast. "Whoa. Dude. Chill. I went for a piss just before you got here. That's why there's footsteps."

The quick cover had the weapon wavering and its holder barking, "Check the truck."

A guy, also in the military-style gear, his snow goggles possibly quipped with night vision, moved to the rear. He didn't return.

"Kevin? What did you find?" the leader yelled.

Kevin didn't reply.

"I'll go check on him. He's probably stuffing his pockets with something." A second fellow sauntered off, leaving only the two. Both were massively distracted, which made this a good time for Raymond to do something monumentally stupid. He grabbed for the wrist with the gun and squeezed, causing the guy to trigger a shot. *Bang.*

In the storm it was loud and muffled all at once.

Louder still the grunts of exertion as he wrestled with the guy, only to gasp when the second assailant clubbed him from behind.

Raymond's ears rang, and he reflexively loosened his hold. His defenses lowered. Fists pummeled him, one two three.

"Argh!" Someone screamed, and the punching stopped.

Opening his eyes, he could only squint at the falling snow. The headlights made it hard to see more than the occasional dark movement within it. It had to be Lainey.

And she needed his help!

He dove for the action and grabbed the asshole about to sucker-punch her, spinning the guy around so that his face could meet his fist. Raymond would have kept punching if a cold voice hadn't said, "Let him go or we shoot the woman."

The threat made Raymond pause. He released the guy he was beating to blink as the headlights splintering the storm outlined the shape of a man striding through the blizzard. He showed no features. His snow goggles and tuque covered almost every inch of his head. His neck gator covered his chin. But there was no mistaking the command in his bearing.

It was Lainey who hissed, "Mr. X!"

The name had Raymond stepping over the thug crumpled on the ground. "You." The only thing that managed to pass Raymond's lips before Lainey screamed, "Die, you bastard!"

She head-butted the guy holding her. Shots fired. One of them shattered the windshield of the truck.

That was the moment Lainey forgot herself and yelled, "Sunshine!"

It caught Mr. X's attention. He held up his hand, and his backup stopped firing. "Who is in the truck?"

"No one." Lainey faced him, eyes black as she stared hard.

Raymond thought he heard a whisper on the wind saying, *On your knees*.

Sounded cold to him so he stood, but one of the new men hit the ground.

A chuckle rumbled from Mr. X. "Your tricks don't work on me. Get her!" As the military-clad dudes moved, so did Raymond.

"Don't you touch her!" Raymond bolted for the X guy, only to hiss in pain as a bullet grazed him, drawing blood.

As if the night didn't have enough coppery scent.

Perhaps that was what drew the vampire child from the shattered windshield of the truck.

Could be she wanted to help her mother.

The reason didn't matter once Sunshine hissed and showed her teeth.

18

Sunshine flew, teeth bared, her eyes a pure black.

Everyone saw it. The moment Lainey feared had arrived. Still, she tried to stop it. "Sunshine, no."

She couldn't see Mr. X's expression, but she imagined it was triumphant as he beheld Sunshine advancing, huffing through her teeth, trying to act tough, but Lainey knew better. Her child was scared and not thinking. She had forgotten all she'd been taught.

Hide. She should have hidden.

"Look at that," Mr. X exclaimed, his excitement discernible despite the head coverings. "You had a child."

"Leave her alone." Lainey started to move. Guns lifted and aimed for her head. She froze.

Sunshine suddenly veered from Mr. X to the nearest guy with a gun. They all ignored her. After all, her baby girl seemed so small. Innocent. Until Sunshine moved so fast no one could stop her. She latched onto a thug's arm, throwing off his aim. His sharp screams filled the air.

Sunshine didn't let go even as he swung, trying to fling her off. On the contrary, Sunshine appeared to be enjoying herself as she suckled.

Another lesson ignored. Lainey had taught her daughter living humans weren't food. But she'd also taught her to fight. To never go quietly because the alternative was worse.

"Sunshine, drop that arm and run!"

Her daughter didn't flee to the woods where she might be safe. Bloodlust and fear had her in its grip and, even better, distracted the other guards, even Mr. X himself. Raymond took advantage and grappled with another gunman.

Another vehicle arrived, and Lainey knew they couldn't win. "Sunshine, now!" she bellowed.

For a moment she thought Sunshine would disobey again. With eyes all black and a mouth lined in red, her daughter tossed Lainey a feral look.

Lainey's heart sank.

Raymond barked, "You heard your mother. Move!"

The eyes lost their wild nature within a blink,

and as if suddenly awake again, Sunshine fled into the snowy woods, Lainey on her heels, while Raymond laid out the guy who thought he'd chase a little girl.

Mr. X remained out of the fight and now taunted, "Call her back before she dies in those woods."

"It would be gentler than what you have planned for her," was her parting shot as she ran, snaring Raymond on her way.

They bolted into the forest and lost all light— along with any sense of direction.

The urge to scream for Sunshine proved almost as painful as the teeth biting her tongue to stay quiet. Bad enough her breath huffed hotly. Her half-vampire ass still required oxygen to live.

Raymond remained by her side, a hand lightly touching the middle of her back as if he were afraid to lose her in this world of darkness. A valid fear. She'd lost Sunshine.

The realization slowed her steps until Lainey stood in a drift of snow. She glanced around and could see nothing. It terrified.

"Raymond?" His name quavered on her lips.

He grabbed her. "I'm here."

He was, but what about her daughter? "Sunshine?"

"I'm sorry. I don't know where she is. I lost her the second she hit the forest."

"Me too," she whispered. "I can't sense her." When Sunshine hid, scent, sight, sound...all of them disappeared. They could have walked right by her and never known.

"Don't panic. We'll find her."

"How?" She couldn't help but cry it.

Before he could reply, the enemy found them. It should have been impossible for humans in this storm, only they weren't human she soon realized. The growling gave it away.

Werewolves working for Mr. X.

One of them burst out of its uniform and snarled at her. Oh jeezus.

She held its slavering teeth away from her face. But could feel it drooling. Then she could see it in a greenish glow as someone cracked a stick of neon light. She met its gaze.

Held it and whispered, "Sleep."

The wolf snarled.

She pushed harder. "*Sleep.*"

The creature blinked.

Sleep.

She pushed everything she had into the command against the strong mind fighting her. She gave too much and passed out.

19

THE THUG'S HEAD CONNECTED WITH A TREE, and he slumped to the ground. In that moment Raymond he realized he couldn't hear anything but the storm. No fighting. No grunts of exertion.

Nothing.

"Lainey?" She didn't reply, and he panicked for a second as he whirled to glance at the stormy forest, lit in an eerie green gloom that illuminated the wolf suddenly diving for him. Raymond managed to put up his arms and divert it, the wet crunch as it hit a spearing limb making him wince.

It wasn't the only dead wolf. He saw a dark shape a few yards away then nothing as the temporary light blinked out.

How would he find Lainey?

Stop. Think. Listen.

He paused and took a deep breath. Another.

Think.

Listen.

Feel.

Over there. He found himself moving quickly, unerringly, as if drawn to Lainey. A lodestone in the storm.

He dropped to his knees when his feet kicked something unmoving but not hard as a rock. He shoved the hairy body to the side with his hands then found Lainey lying in the snow, unmoving. For a moment he panicked as he dragged her into his arms, a woman he barely knew, and yet she already meant so much to him.

Unable to see, he palpated her for damage and found nothing. However, Lainey appeared possessed of a deep tremble. Had she succumbed to the cold?

He needed to get her somewhere warm, protected.

Slinging her over his shoulder, keeping one hand free, he trudged through the forest. The goggles he'd scooped off a body helped him to find his way, but it was his nose scenting something that drew him to the overhang that led to a shallow cave.

He tucked Lainey as deep as he could before he left to see if he could find anything to start a fire with. He snapped icy branches and brought them into the crevice. They were damp, but with the dried debris that had drifted into the cave he made a decent pile just inside the mouth. The matches Sunshine had given him made perfect sense now. It took three before he managed to light some leaves and the dry branch nestled within them.

The enemy might spot it, but it was a chance he took in case there was a little girl watching. Thinking of her had him eyeing the opening to the cave. Should he be out there looking for her? He crouched in the mouth of the cave, only to hear Lainey softly say, "Sunshine doesn't mind the cold. It's not as dangerous to her as it is to us."

He turned to look at her. "There's other perils. She's so little."

"I know."

"And alone." He glanced outside.

"She's been taught how to survive in case we ever got separated." Spoken on a broken note.

He moved to her and drew her into his lap. "We'll find her. I swear."

"I hope so. I need my Sunshine."

"I know." He hugged her and noticed the trembling hadn't abated. "You're freezing."

"It's because I need to rest. Mesmerizing takes a lot out of me. My battery is running low."

"You need blood?" He held out his arm immediately. "Have some of mine."

"I can't."

"Why not? I'm sure it's very tasty."

They couldn't see much of each other with the low flames of the fire, but he imagined her smile as she replied, "I know you're delicious."

"Then bite me."

"I can't. I have a rule."

"Is this some *Pretty Woman* kind of thing? You don't have to kiss me to get it." He shoved up his sleeve, exposing his forearm.

"I don't eat from live people."

"So you like corpses?" He wrinkled his nose.

"No!" she hotly exclaimed. "I get the blood in other ways. Blood banks. Ads in the paper. People will sell anything. And we can do animal blood. It's just a more pungent flavor."

"We have none of that here with us. Just fresh from the source." He shook his arm.

She sighed. "You're pushy.

"And you're being stubborn. You need it. I have it. Take it."

"You're not making this very appealing," she grumbled.

"Is that your way of saying you want my neck?"

"Or your thigh. I'm partial to both."

"So I should take off my pants?"

"I appreciate the offer, but it's too cold." She shivered in his arms again.

He turned her in his grip and cupped her head to press her face to his neck. "Drink."

He half expected her to argue again. Instead, her lips latched to the skin. She sucked and teased at him, giving him a massive erection.

When she finally did bite, his hips thrust in pleasure, and it seemed only natural for his hands to slip past the waistband of her pants to find her slit. Wet. Willing. She rocked against his hand as he fingered her.

He thrust in time to her suckling. Felt himself getting harder and harder. When she released his neck, he could have yelled his frustration, only her hands pulled at his pants, unbuckled him. He shoved hers down far enough he could flip her onto her back, push up her legs, and thrust into her.

She cried out, and he moved by instinct alone. Seesawed into her, her sex gripping him tight, her pants his encouragement.

When she came on his cock, pulsing and milking him, he went to pull out, only to have her beg him, "No. Stay. Come inside me."

How could he say no? He climaxed hard, spilling his seed. The first time without protection, ever.

He wanted to be selfish and stay inside her all night, but her skin remained chilly. He quickly had her pants back in place. Then insisted on tucking his coat around her, too, despite her protests.

"I'm fine. That fire is making me hot."

Curled around her, he fell asleep, only to later wake sweating while she remained shivering cold. He stripped and gave her his clothes before wrapping himself around her again. This cuddling thing was nice. So nice, he practically purred with contentment before falling asleep.

He was startled awake by a voice squeaking, "Mommy, you found a giant Floofkins."

20

SUNSHINE'S VOICE WOKE LAINEY, AND SHE raised her head from the warm, furry pillow.

Wait.

What furry pillow?

Within the faint glow from the dying fire she realized she was cushioned against a very large cat. A lynx to be exact. It twitched and rumbled as he stared with one eye at her daughter. Her smart Sunshine had found them.

And it appeared she and Raymond had found the den of a large cat.

"Um, baby girl, you might want to back up." And where was Raymond?

"But I want to pet da kitty." Sunshine plopped herself down and stroked a hand over the cat, who rumbled again.

"Nice kitty," Lainey muttered as she sat up. As she blinked away the last of sleep, it hit her.

The cat was Raymond.

But how?

Didn't he need catnip?

"Raymond is that you?" she asked.

The man—er, cat—sat up and gazed at himself with curiosity, lifted one paw, then the other. Stood and looked between his four legs. Even wiggled the nub on his butt.

"Rowr?" He sounded questioning.

She couldn't help but stroke a hand down his back as she said, "Yes, you appear to be a lynx."

"I'm gonna call him Floofkins Two," Sunshine announced.

The very idea made Lainey laugh. "Don't be silly, baby girl. This kitty already has a name. It's Raymond."

"Daddy?" Then more excitedly. "Daddy is a big kitty." Predictably, little girl arms wound around his neck, but he bore it, and even head-butted Sunshine to her giggling delight.

Rising in a half-crouch to accommodate the cave, Lainey noticed the cooling embers of the fire he'd built. Then recalled what else he'd done to keep her warm.

His blood had been pure ecstasy, with the sex being the delicious dessert on top. Her cheeks could have melted all the snow, given how hot they suddenly turned at the recollection. What was it about Raymond that had her acting out of character?

Sex should have been the last thing on her mind last night, and yet, when her lips met his skin, it turned erotic right away. Not something that usually happened. Hell, she usually mocked movies that portrayed vampires eating a meal as if it were porn.

Last night, for the first time, it had turned triple X-rated. She'd been orgasming practically the entire time she sucked at him while he fingered her.

Raymond nudged her, and she would have sworn his gaze said he knew exactly what she was thinking of.

Dear gawd, could he smell it?

She distracted herself by asking her daughter, "Where did you go? We lost you in the woods."

"I found a hole in a tree and hid until the bad man left."

"Mr. X is gone?"

Sunshine nodded.

"You're sure?" Lainey asked.

"Yup."

"This is our chance to get out of here before he comes back." Glancing at her watch, Lainey frowned. "We've got only three hours until dawn."

The lynx cocked his head, as if asking something.

She would have sworn she heard him. "In clear

conditions, we'd be about forty-five minutes from the city. But first we have to find the road, not that it helps fix the truck situation. Maybe we'll be lucky and someone will come by soon. I might be able to find a tow truck." She couldn't help a dubious note.

"Bad man car."

"What?" Lainey blinked at Sunshine. "Did you say batman car?"

Her daughter shook her head. "Bad," she enunciated. "We take the bad man car."

"Are you saying there's a vehicle on the road we can use?"

Sunshine nodded. "And I gots a key!" A fob dangled from her kid's finger suddenly.

Asking how or when her child got it might open a Pandora's box she'd rather keep closed. Lainey glanced at Raymond. "We need to get out of here. Are you staying on four legs or getting dressed?" She held up his clothes.

The big lynx uttered a meow of frustration.

"Sunshine, give me a second with Raymond. I think he needs help getting back to himself."

"You gonna give him a kiss like da frog?" Someone had recently been on a fairy tale binge.

Lainey's lips quirked as she quipped, "I just might."

Sunshine giggled as she slipped out of the cave,

and Lainey turned her attention to the lynx. "Thanks for keeping me warm last night."

"Rowr-rowr."

"That's a nice-looking cat you've got."

"Miaow."

"I need you as a man now, though."

"Grawr." Impatience shone in the sound.

"You switched without thinking about it. Now shift back."

He made an annoyed growling noise again. On impulse she grabbed his fur and rubbed her nose to his. "Can't kiss me without lips. Can't touch me without fingers. Can't make me come unless you're a man," she whispered.

The strangest sensation tingled her fingers and nose. Her closed eyes missed seeing him morph from cat to man, but she recognized the feel of those lips on hers. Might have kissed him longer if a little voice hadn't once more interrupted to say, "Why Daddy naked?"

21

Raymond couldn't get dressed fast enough once Sunshine interrupted. And icy water didn't shrivel half as much as a child that stared. He might never find his dick again.

A thought quickly lost with one glance at Lainey. Around her he endured a perpetual semi-hard-on. Even now, a bit ragged around the edges, she was confidant, determined, and beautiful. Her pallor, almost glowing in the dying embers of his fire, made him wonder if he should offer more blood.

"You hungry?" he asked.

It was Sunshine who first replied. "I ate."

He didn't ask her what or who.

Lainey pursed her lips. "I'm good. We should move before Mr. X sends more mercenaries after us."

Pointing out that those mercs might already be

waiting seemed counterproductive. It wasn't as if they could stay in this nice cozy cave forever.

They trudged back to the road single file, following a child who chattered as she skipped. The storm had waned, and now a deep chill filled the land, the kind that frosted his breath and rimmed his eyelashes with ice. The sky remained dark. It was the deepest, darkest hour of night, and yet Sunshine danced as she moved. She didn't make a sound, and yet her every motion held a joy. Lainey's posture remained taut and alert. Every step was cautious and involved a rotation of her head, as if she could see in the dark. Maybe she could.

Raymond only barely missed slamming into trees or rattling branches. His enhanced sight required at least a tiny amount of light.

Not a sound marred their journey other than the creak of rubbing limbs and the inexplicable noise of snow compacting. As they moved single file and cautiously, his mind wandered, trying to catch up with everything that had happened.

He'd had sex with Lainey again. Epic sex that came after enjoying—seriously enjoying—his first vampire bite. Probably not his last so long as Lainey did the chomping.

Then, during the night he'd turned into a cat without needing catnip. Instead, he'd had a dream. A dream he was running on four legs and living the life of a lynx.

The shock of waking up a cat had faded to curiosity. Could he change into his feline again? He'd certainly returned to his man shape easily enough. He'd expected pain at the very least, despite what his brothers claimed. Instead, it was as if he'd stretched and popped his joints.

The sensation was good, not bad.

As a matter of fact, despite the fact he was trudging in the woods, freezing his 'nads off, he felt great. He wouldn't trade this for anything. All he wanted was to be there for the woman he loved.

He almost fell face first in the snow as his thoughts casually tossed that in there.

Love.

Hell yeah.

This wild and crazy feeling for Lainey could be nothing else.

The urge filled him to shout it aloud and let her know. She might just murder him if he did, this not being the time and place for those kinds of declarations.

Once they got safe, and she could relax, then he'd tell her how he felt.

Maybe.

What if she didn't feel the same? What if she rejected him? Laughed?

Fuck.

As if sensing his stare, she glanced over her shoulder and mouthed, *What's wrong?*

Did he tell her about his revelation?

Nope. His soundless reply? *Gotta pee.*

Only a partial lie. He could have held it but instead ducked behind a tree. Couldn't let her see him being crazy. No way she'd believe he loved her this soon. They'd just met.

He had a hard time himself, and yet having heard about it and seen it in movies and books, he finally understood how quickly it could happen with the right person. He now had scientific proof love at first sight existed.

Her voice from the other side of the trunk startled him. "Hurry up. Dawn is coming."

Stage fright made it hard to force it out, and when he emerged from his hiding spot, she didn't help with a smirk that he only saw because of the gleam of her teeth. "Took you long enough."

"It's cold," he muttered.

"I had no problem." For some reason the thought of her peeing flustered.

"We're not far now from the truck," she said, not noticing his silence. "I don't sense anything. You?"

He shook his head and added a soft, "Nope."

It turned out they closer to the road than expected. They emerged from the forest to find the truck still on its side, buried in at least a foot of snow. The abandoned vehicle on the shoulder wasn't any better, but it started right away with the keys Sunshine had filched. While he cleared the windows and roof, Lainey went to grab their stuff. Since the SUV had an open trunk area, she used blankets to quickly create a dark tent.

In the console between the front seats, he located a cellphone in the cupholder. Locked, of course, but showing the last text message on the screen.

Coordinates for Lainey's place, which he knew because he'd memorized them. She'd been right to burn the house down.

He tucked the phone into his pocket for later and poked his head in the back to see if the girls needed help. Sunshine was in a nest of bags with a blanket stretched over top, goggles and mask in her lap ready to be worn.

She waved at him. "No more moose."

A grin pulled his lips. "I hope that's a prediction. Good job, by the way, on getting those keys."

"You welcome." Sunshine beamed.

"We ready to go?" he asked Lainey, who'd done a last trip to the truck and emerged with the cooler she'd put into the trunk.

"Yeah, but we need to move fast," she announced. "Chances are they left their car behind in the hopes of using it to flush us out."

Meaning they'd be on the lookout. Despite knowing that, they didn't have much choice. They couldn't go on foot. "We'll ditch it soon as we can."

"Actually, a quicker solution is me disabling the on-board GPS system so they can't track the signal." She had already tossed her laptop into the front seat.

"Or we could send them in the wrong direction instead." He'd seen it done in the movies.

The suggestion put a big smile on Lainey's lips. "It's evil. I like it."

With her tapping away, Raymond had to drive, which he would never admit daunted. His most recent snow driving experience was of the video game kind. Not exactly the same.

He had to take his time on the road not yet cleared by plows. Slow going didn't describe it. He kept his gaze peeled for signs of traffic. Eventually they encountered a single set of tire tracks forging the way and made better time. The sky lightened as the dawn came with blinding brilliance, refracting off the freshly fallen snow.

It forced Sunshine to put on the mask and goggles then hide under blankets, but not without protest. "Mommy, I wanna see."

"I am not having you turn into a lobster because it's sunny out."

"Hate dis." Sunshine sighed with exaggeration that might be a precursor to her teen years.

He hoped to be around for them.

Their plan as they entered the city was simple but dangerous now that dawn had hit. It required he find a hotel with a covered portico to protect Sunshine as much as they could from daylight. Lainey had him going in circles to reach one, guiding him via streets lacking camera surveillance.

Since it didn't have online check-in, Raymond registered in person, looking like a bum but able to secure a room since he still had his wallet and credit card. Fake ones, of course, that wouldn't lead back to his family. He could only hope Mr. X hadn't managed to identify him from the snowstorm fight. He paid extra for valet service as well so he wouldn't have to deal with the car.

He'd rented adjoining rooms on the second floor. They were standard fare for this type of chain motel with a pair of double beds in each room. A desk with a chair. Television on a long dresser.

Lainey immediately went for the windows and pulled the blackout drapes before she began to seal any sunlit seams shut with the roll of tape she pulled from her knapsack. Only once she'd secured the room did she allow Sunshine to strip.

The kid sighed as the layers peeled off. "Whew. I hate wearing dat."

"Someone looks tired," Lainey said. "I think you should go to bed."

"Okay." The kid didn't even argue. "I eat first? Hungry."

"Shit. Yeah. Of course."

Lainey thawed and warmed the blood in the microwave, and Sunshine hummed as she drank it. Her eyes drooped right after, and Raymond was there to grab her before she fell asleep sitting on the edge of the bed. He lifted her while Lainey pulled back the covers. Placing her against the sheets, he didn't expect the sleepy hug and sloppy kiss.

"Night, Daddy."

"Night, princess." It emerged gruff. He stepped aside as Lainey moved in.

"You were a brave girl. A smart one. You did good," Lainey praised, stroking stray strands of hair from Sunshine's face.

"I bit dat man," lisped the little girl.

"You had no choice. You saved our lives. And saved yourself."

"It was bad."

"No, baby girl." Lainey gathered the child into her arms. "Never bad. You had to do it. That man would have hurt you."

"But Mommy, I liked it." The true worry emerged, and Sunshine glanced upward at Lainey.

At the door between the rooms, Raymond paused, half tempted to storm back and tell Sunshine she had nothing to feel guilty about.

However, he wasn't her dad. Lainey, though, knew just what to say.

"I'm gonna tell you a secret, baby girl. I like biting people, too. The important thing is to only bite those who are evil."

"Like da bad man."

"Exactly."

Simple, but true. Raymond would have never thought himself capable of harming anyone until that attack in the snowstorm. It was fight or die. Turned out, he could battle if needed.

He left the hotel's adjoining room door open in case they needed him. He truly expected Lainey to stay with Sunshine in the other bed, so imagine his surprise when she entered his room and shut the door most of the way before she flopped onto the bed beside him.

He froze, afraid movement would send her fleeing.

"What a fucking night," she sighed.

"No shit."

She glanced over at him. "Thank you for everything you did."

"You mean like leading Mr. X to you?" The coincidence of his arrival and the timing of Mr. X's arrival were too big to ignore.

"Not entirely your fault." Her nose wrinkled. "Given how easily you found me, it was only a matter of time."

"Easy?" He snorted.

She offered a mischievous grin. "Aren't you glad you made the effort?"

She meant it as a joke, but he replied in all seriousness, "Very glad I found you."

As if suddenly shy, she glanced away from him. "Think we're safe for the next few minutes? I'd kill for a shower."

"I'll stand guard." And fantasize about her naked body being sluiced by water.

"Or you could scrub my back."

The invitation was casual, and he wondered if she meant it since she rose from the bed and headed for the bathroom. She left the door open, and a moment later, her clothes came flying out.

Definitely an invite.

He glanced at the adjoining door, left open a crack. As if she read his mind, Lainey said, "She's out cold from exhaustion and will probably sleep hard for a few hours at least."

He needed no further encouragement. His clothes hit the floor, and in moments, he was standing behind her in the tub-shower combo, the plastic curtain pulled across holding in the steam.

She stood under the spray, head back, hair slicked, body wet, and finally her body was his to see in its entirety. Breasts that begged cupping. Nipples that wanted sucking. Indented waist and hips he'd held on to.

She draped her arms around him as he stood stupidly staring and drew him close. "Where's my kiss?" she demanded.

Right here. Right now. He embraced her with a hunger that only seemed to grow the more he got to know her. He tasted her lips. Sucked on her tongue. But he wanted more than that. He worshipped those nipples, tugging and biting on the hardened nubs.

He palmed them in his hands, massaging and teasing until she growled, "Stop toying with me."

"It's called worship." And it came in so many forms, like him dropping to his knees that he might part her thighs and lap at her.

Her back hit the shower wall, her leg went over his shoulder, and she succumbed to his licking. But the best part was her coming around his fingers when he thrust them in time to flicks of his tongue on her clit.

While in the midst of her orgasmic aftershocks, she turned around and waggled her bottom. "Take me. Now."

He needed no further encouragement. He stood, and his hard cock slid into her. Pure heaven. The tight fit of her squeezed, and he had to grit his teeth to prolong the pleasure long enough that she panted for a second time. Still thrusting, he reached under and fondled her clit until her body tensed, and she gasped hard as she climaxed.

"Fuck." The word burst from him as her sex fisted and made him come. The pleasure was so intense he was the one biting down on the flesh of her shoulder hard enough to break skin.

He was pretty sure in the midst of his pleasure she orgasmed a third time. All he knew was by the time he came down from the high, their skin was getting wrinkly and he wanted nothing more than to be with this woman.

They made it to the bed where they spooned in a mess of limbs and slept.

Nothing spelled good morning—or was that evening—than having a child say, "Me snuggle, too."

22

"No, you cannot snuggle us," Lainey hotly exclaimed, very much aware she and Raymond were very naked and intertwined under the comforter.

"Daddy naked 'gain?" Sunshine cocked her head.

"I was, um, hot." Raymond ducked under the sheet, trying to hide his ruddy cheeks.

Lainey almost giggled until her kid said, "Mommy, where your jammies? I see boobies."

Her turn for fiery cheeks despite the fact she wasn't a blusher. She'd had things done to her that had jaded her to all things innocent in the world. Until it came to Raymond. With him she felt shy, uncertain, bold, and passionate. A dichotomy she'd yet to resolve.

She'd gone into his room knowing she wanted

sex with him. She with the low drive when it came to bodily pleasure practically pounced, and it had been the best thing she'd ever experienced.

It made her finally understand what the big deal was when it came to sex. The clumsy quick fumblings she'd participated in while a prisoner were nothing compared to what she felt with Raymond.

"How did you sleep?" she asked as she noticed her shirt on the floor across the room. Out of reach, which meant flashing some tits if she wanted to grab it.

"Slept good," Sunshine declared, hopping onto the bed, and by the look of panic on Raymond's face, it was a close call.

"How do you feel?" she asked. Sunshine had endured a strenuous attack. It would have taken a toll physically as well as mentally.

"I'm hungry." Sunshine bounced as she rubbed her tummy, and Raymond scooched until he sat with his back against the headboard, more concerned about his family jewels than the modesty of his chest.

Trust Sunshine to notice and point. "Why Daddy got lines?"

It took a Lainey a second to realize her kid spoke of the muscle delineation. Raymond was pretty damned fit. And sexy. Mmm.

"Why don't you put on some cartoons while I get dressed?" Lainey said.

"Toons!" With one last attempt to maim Raymond, Sunshine bounced off the bed and bolted into the other room.

Raymond stared at the door. "Is it safe to get out of bed?"

"Probably not, man with lines." Lainey patted his abs. "Get used to having no privacy. Kids have no boundaries when they're young."

It was only as he stared at her that she realized what she'd done. Implied he'd be around.

His smile melted everything inside her. "Guess I better get used to sleeping in a jock."

Apparently, he didn't mind the idea of sticking around. And she didn't know how she felt about it.

Flustered, she ran for her bag of clothes then the bathroom.

A cold wet facecloth helped to cool down her embarrassment. By the time she emerged, it was to find Raymond chatting with Sunshine, heating up a bag of blood and then mixing it with the instant porridge. He served it to her with a juice box he'd already poked a straw into, talking and gesturing as he told a story.

Being a dad.

It hit her hard. Especially seeing how Sunshine responded to him. She'd been so busy keeping her daughter a secret that she'd forgotten just how lonely it could be living sequestered. Lainey had escaped one prison, only to create one of her own making and she'd forced her daughter to live in it.

Something had to change. This couldn't go on. Sunshine deserved a chance at a life.

"I need to go out for a bit," Lainey said suddenly before ducking her head into the cooler, looking for something to eat.

"Where? Do we need to pack up? Or are we coming back?""

She rose with a frozen protein shake. "Sunshine can't go out. It won't be dark for another two hours at least. We can't wait that long. We need to dump the vehicle and make arrangements for travel."

Immediately Raymond offered, "I'll go."

"And where will you go? You don't know the city like I do. Plus, I know where to get another car."

He didn't need to be clubbed with the logic. "Guess it makes more sense for you to go."

"I won't be long." She hoped as she layered on a jacket and her boots.

As she prepared to leave, Sunshine threw herself at her, her arms hugging her tight. "Wuv you."

"I love you, too, baby girl." Her throat tightened, and her voice had a raspy quality as she added, "You be a good girl for Raymond."

"Yes, Mommy." Sunshine nodded.

And then it was Raymond pulling Lainey into his grip and murmuring against her ear, "Be careful."

"I always am." It was only as she strode down the hall that she amended that to always was. She'd gotten tired of being careful. All it did was make her life not much different than before.

And that was why she'd lied to the daughter who meant the most to her in the world and the man who was rapidly gaining the same distinction. They might not understand she didn't have a choice. Raymond would have insisted on coming, but Sunshine couldn't be left alone.

As to where she was going? When she'd played with the stolen car's GPS, the log files for it showed all kinds of trips in and around the city, all of them eventually returning to one address. Looking it up, she'd discovered it wasn't far, and while she could find no images or information, it was definitely a place of interest, given her quick research revealed the owner of it buried amidst shell companies.

She'd only brought her large purse containing the things you expected a woman with a child to have—if you ignored the explosives made to look like children's clay stuffed in a box appropriated from a dollar store.

By now, despite all her fancy screwing with the GPS, Mr. X knew they'd not taken the stolen vehicle to Nunavut. Had he returned to the address she found in the GPS? A place so close to her last home it filled her veins with ice.

How many times had she passed an Xlab employee in the street? She must not have ever crossed paths with Mr. X himself, or he'd have found her much sooner than this.

Ironic really, how she'd ended up in a city with one of Mr. X's facilities. None of the records she'd stolen and sifted through from the other labs had ever hinted at one in Alaska. Could she have been wrong?

It took forty-five minutes to get there usually, over an hour and a half by being careful and making sure she didn't acquire a tail. The address belonged to a sprawling mansion outside the city with a long, two-car-wide driveway lined in pine trees. At the end was a massive house built of stone and cedar. She drove past the closed iron wrought gates, clenching the steering wheel.

Holy shit. She'd not expected to find a home. Did it belong to Mr. X?

More than ever, she had to know. Lainey parked well past the estate boundary and hopefully any cameras as she debated what to do.

Darkness wouldn't fall for over another half-hour. Could she afford to wait? A glance at the gleaming snow made her sigh. She'd be much too visible against it. If she didn't want to be caught, she'd have to cool her heels a while longer.

But she didn't have to be idle. She might not have brought her laptop, but her phone could do some basic stuff like scan for Bluetooth signals commonly used by wireless cameras. What it wouldn't detect was the motion sensing kind that saved to an SD card. She'd have to hope that if her picture was taken by one, no one would see it until after she'd done what she'd come to do.

Darkness fell while she got ready, tucking her hair inside a woolen cap, putting on gloves with touch screen fingers, holstering the gun she'd packed even as she hated it. Not liking the weapon didn't mean she didn't know how to use it.

She glanced overhead at the snow-laden boughs as she got out of the car. A jump and grab of a branch sent powdery white stuff dumping, making the car harder to see. Maybe even give the impression it had been there a while.

Keeping to the cover of the trees, she back-tracked, finding the property by locating the fence. She saw no sign of cameras, and her phone app showed no sign of activity. Still, just in case, despite the fact it would eat her battery, she had it send out a disruptive pulse. If there were wireless cameras, they would glitch as she passed through, the blip short-lived to anyone watching and hopefully passing unnoticed.

There were no signs of security, not even any trails. Then again, this far from the main house they might not worry as much. Closer to the mansion, she expected things would get more difficult.

The fence—wrought iron bars topped with spears —posed no challenge. The sun hadn't quite set, which was why she took her time moving through the forest on the inside of the mansion's property.

The snow, while not entirely pristine with its rabbit hops and bird claws, definitely showed the signs of her passage. As long as no one noticed and raised a warning, she would be fine. It didn't appear as if anyone patrolled this area. A piece of luck that only convinced her even more she followed the right plan. Get close to the house. See who lived here. If it had anything to do with Mr. X or his labs, set the explosives and haul ass out of there—while not thinking of the collateral damage to life. It was all about perspective. Sunshine's life against the life of anyone working for Mr. X. The clear winner meant Lainey would also be watching for stragglers and would worry about compassion another day.

She waited at the edge of the woods, visibility difficult already as night gripped the land. She'd yet to see any signs of security other than the fence. It made her wonder if she'd misjudged. Perhaps this place wasn't nefarious at all. In her experience, Mr. X's paranoia led to him investing in some very high-tech security, none of which was apparent here.

Several windows on the main floor and a pair on the second level were illuminated. Someone was home. She edged out of the shielding protection of the trees to traverse a broad expanse of snow, untouched until her arrival. She prickled with awareness. Despite the lack of light, she remained fully aware she stood in the open. If someone watched…

No warning sounded, and she moved quickly, making it to the back of the house with its cleared patio and tarped furniture. Only a hot tub, tightly sealed with steps leading to it, appeared snow free.

The patio door at the far end spilled light onto the icy patio stones. Lainey aimed for the dark French doors. A cautious turn of the handle showed it unlocked.

She almost turned around right then and there. This was too easy.

No way Mr. X lived there. He'd never leave his doors open. He'd have motion-sensing lights. Alarms.

She inspected it for wires. Perhaps it was the kind that wouldn't go off until she opened it. She saw nothing. Swinging open the door didn't set off an alarm, nor did bars slam down.

More and more she wondered if she was mistaken.

The room held only the scent of leather-bound books. A library of some sort. Perhaps even an office given the large desk flanked by the plush chairs on wheels. Her hands skimmed the surface looking for something, anything that would give her a clue of the owner. There were no framed photographs. Nothing of a personal nature. She gnashed her teeth in frustration.

What should she do? Set the bombs and go? And if this place belonged to an innocent? Perhaps the address in the car's guidance system had nothing to do with Mr. X and his henchmen.

She chewed her lip before moving to the wooden door leading farther into the house. This early in the evening, people would still be awake.

She pressed an ear to the closed portal and listened.

Nothing. Just in case, she remained still a while longer.

This place was a dud. She should leave and return to Sunshine and Raymond.

She moved toward the patio entrance, only to freeze as she saw the yard illuminate.

Uh-oh.

An even bigger uh-oh was the sudden barking of a dog outside. In moments it growled and snapped at the door. It wouldn't be long before someone noticed. She bolted for the door that would lead into the house and perhaps a place to hide until she could sneak out of it.

Only when she opened the door to see the welcoming committee did she realize how well she'd been played.

She hissed and stared at the first face she saw. "Sleep." She shouted the command at him, only to see he wore earplugs. They all did, along with goggles, because they were expecting her.

The darts hit her. As her knees buckled and her muscles refused to cooperate, she could only blink at the sight of Mr. X sauntering casually up the hall, wearing his metal mask, hands shoved into his pockets, casual like.

The last thing she heard before she sank into a familiar drugged stupor was his gloating voice. "Hello, VX31. So kind of you to drop in."

23

Two hours after Lainey left, Raymond came to the realization he'd made a mistake in letting her go alone. Something had happened. His anxiety screamed that she needed his help. But what could he do? Going to look for Lainey would mean leaving Sunshine alone. He might have met Lainey only a short while ago, but he knew she'd rather be tortured than leave her child unprotected.

Meaning he was stuck.

Unless... What if someone he trusted could keep an eye on Sunshine? But who? He was in freaking Alaska. Everyone he knew was at least a fourteen-plus-hour plane trip away. That was thirteen hours and fifty-nine minutes too long.

Argh. There must be something he could do other than sit around worrying.

He made a phone call, and his mom picked up on the first ring. "Hello?"

She sounded tentative. With good reason. The burner phone would have come up on her call display with a phone number linked to a popular restaurant chain. "Hey, Mom, it's me."

"Raymond!" She sounded so happy, and it was nice for the three seconds it lasted before she got mad. "Where the heck are you? Almost three days you've been gone without a word. Do you know how worried we've all been?"

The guilt hit him hard. He'd been so determined to sneak up on PinkLlama, he'd left only a three-line note to his family. *Gone to fix stuff. Will call if I can. Water my plants.* Which, in retrospect, was kind of sparse.

"Sorry, Mom. I kind of got caught up in something."

"Are you okay? We didn't know what to think since you disappeared and then didn't send any kind of word." She layered the guilt.

"Sorry." He apologized again. "Things got complicated." And he would have told her all about the woman who confused him and her cute kid, only the situation called for haste. "I need your help."

"Are you in trouble?"

"I'm not but a friend of mine is." Friend. How trite. For once his anxiety wasn't about him but someone else. Someone not related to him. A woman who had made him emerge from his comfort zone and desire more from life.

"A friend? I'm intrigued. I can't wait to hear all about them."

"I don't really have time to go into details." His voice rose for a second, loud enough he glanced at the door between the rooms. He didn't want Sunshine seeing him worried. "I called because I was wondering if you know anyone trustworthy in Alaska."

"As a matter of fact, I do," she said just as someone knocked, not on his door but that of the adjoining room.

He quickly slid through the partition. Sunshine glanced up from her coloring book. He put a finger to his lips.

"I gotta call you back," he whispered to his mom.

"Answer the door," Mom replied as the sharp rap came again. It oddly echoed through his phone. He stared at it then the portal to the hall.

No way.

He moved slowly to the door, only to startle as Sunshine said, "It's okay. It's Grandma."

"What?" He almost tripped over his own two feet he pivoted so fast.

"Grandma. See." Lainey held up the picture she'd drawn of a rotund, curly-haired woman wearing red and a bunch of stick people at her back. One sported orange hair on the top and bottom of the circle head.

No fucking way.

Raymond flung open the door and gaped at a portion of his family. There was his mom, brothers Dominick and Stefan, along with Nimway, Stefan's girlfriend.

"What are you doing here?" he exclaimed.

"I told you we were worried," Mom said, looking like a giant target in her big red parka. "When we realized you were gone, Nimway had the Valley Pack Hub"—basically the brains of the wolf pack's security team—"check for your location. You didn't make it easy."

"I was trying to be incognito." He'd used a fake passport and matching credit card to travel. "How did you track me down?"

"They ran your face against security video footage. Which took way too much time," Mom declared.

"No fucking kidding. You should have heard Mom bitching," Stefan complained.

"It wasn't all bad. She baked a ton of stuff." Dominick patted his belly.

Mom's chin lifted. "Neither of you are funny. As to how we got here, the moment their facial recognition software triggered at the airport, we tracked down your flight and jumped on the next plane."

"And you brought a posse?" Raymond drawled as he gazed upon the crowd in the hall. It appeared a few of the Valley Pack had also joined them.

"We weren't sure what kind of help you might need, so we went for overkill," Stefan offered with a shrug.

His family had come to his rescue. It made a guy feel warm. "I'm glad you're here."

"Me too!" Sunshine chirped. She'd snuck up behind him while he dealt with his mom and family in the hall.

Her arrival narrowed Mom's gaze. "And who is this?"

"I'm Sunshine."

"And her mom, Lainey, is the friend I was telling you about on the phone." Would his mom grasp that he didn't want to say anything in front of the child?

"Hello, Sunshine."

"Hi." The kid suddenly turned shy and lifted her arms. He grabbed her and tucked her onto his hip. Her arms looped around him as she leaned her head trustingly against him.

Mom noticed, and for a second, he worried he might have given her a heart attack. She swayed and gasped. "Raymond, what's going on? Whose child is this?"

While time was of the essence, he knew he'd have to tell his family something. "Get inside and

I'll tell you about Lainey. We met in an online game."

"Did we seriously fly fifteen hours because Raymond got a girlfriend?" Stefan exclaimed.

"It involves Mr. X."

That shut them all up, and everyone came inside except for Nimway's squad of wolves in human clothing. She sent them out to secure stairwells and the outside of the hotel.

Once the door closed, his family demanded answers. It didn't take long to get them up to speed. His brothers snickered at Lainey finding him in a video game. Their jaws dropped as they heard the story of the snowstorm and then the fight. Their eyes rounded when he explained the importance of not only of hiding Sunshine but keeping her out of daylight. And finally, Lainey's disappearance.

He wasn't exactly crazy about telling them the whole story in front of Sunshine, but for one, she'd lived it. Most importantly, she'd insisted on remaining in his arms and wouldn't let go.

At the end of his story, Stefan exhaled. "Shit." Glanced at Sunshine and stammered, "I mean, damn, um, f—fudge."

It made Nimway snicker. "It's a curse word. It won't kill the kid. I'm sure she's heard it before."

"People aren't supposed to swear in front of kids," Stefan muttered.

"It's not a big deal." Nimway's reply.

"Not a big deal?" Stefan huffed. "Does this mean you'll swear in front of ours?"

"Who says we're having any?" Nimway countered.

"I insist on at least one."

"Pussy. I was thinking at least three or four." His girlfriend turned the tables, and Stefan's jaw hit the floor.

Sunshine said nothing, but Raymond felt her mirth.

Mom beamed. "Bring me all the grandbabies."

"Can you ooh and aah over these imaginary children later? I need to figure out how to find and help Lainey," Raymond finally interrupted.

"You don't know she's in trouble."

"Bad man has her." At Sunshine's declaration, his blood ran cold while his family looked at her oddly.

It left Raymond to explain. "Sunshine's not just a vampire; she's also psychic."

The statement had Mom's gaze veering to the picture on the bed. The rotund stick person on it wearing red like her. "Sweetheart, why don't we go have ourselves some girl-time. No boys allowed." She held out her hand.

Sunshine slid from his lap and took two steps before stopping to glance back at Raymond. "What about my daddy?"

Mom blinked and said nothing, but Dominick did. "Holy shit. Congrats, Raymond."

Mom wasn't as delicate. "Raymond Francis Hubbard. What the hell?"

"I'm not her actual father, but Sunshine's decided she'd like me to be." He didn't add the part about how he wouldn't mind being her dad.

Mom glanced between them. "Blood or not, there's obviously a bond between you."

"Yes." He didn't even try to deny it. "And that's why I need to go find her mom."

"Who might have been taken by Mr. X. Our biggest enemy," Stefan clarified.

"Most likely. And if that's the case, all the more reason to go after him. We won't be safe until he's gone."

"Your brother is right," Nimway remarked. "So long as Mr. X knows of us, we will always be in danger. It's time we handled this."

"That's my family. Working together to keep us all safe." Mom beamed. "I know you'll find a way."

Only as his mom left, with Sunshine saying, "Grandma, do you like to draw?" did his brothers pounce.

Dominick first. "Dude, when I said get laid, I meant with a living, breathing person, not a vampire."

"Lainey's not dead. Not even close." And even if

she was, he didn't care because she made his blood run hot.

His vehement reply had Stefan gaping. "Holy fuck, he's banging the vampire chick."

"She's not a chick or a real vampire. She's like us. Someone who didn't ask for this kind of life. Lainey just wants to be safe and happy."

"And what little brother wants, we help get." Dominick glanced at Stefan. "Now I see why Mom never let us beat the snot out of those bullies when he was a kid. She was saving us for this moment."

"Mom wouldn't let you beat them up because you would have gotten expelled." Raymond rolled his eyes.

"Bah. Would have been worth it. Never was good at the school thing." Dominick had said all through high school his only choice was the military as a grunt. The world needed more awkward people like Raymond, who were book smart. It needed the courageous like Dominick, who knew how to fight, and the cunning like Stefan, who said, "Do we know where to start looking?"

"No, but I've got an idea." He pulled out the phone he'd found in the car. "We're going to need to steal a computer." Because he didn't know the password to Lainey's, and it had locked him out after two wrong attempts.

"It's after nine. The stores are all closed," Dominick remarked.

Stefan laughed. "The people with the kind of equipment we want don't keep regular hours."

And even better, Raymond's brother knew how to find them.

24

Lainey woke inside a room-sized glass box with frosted panes. She wasn't wearing her clothes but a two-piece medical outfit. Scrub pants and top. No shoes, just socks. She blinked. Her eyes felt dry and gritty. The reason, she quickly discovered, being the contact lenses adhering to her irises. She wouldn't be able to mesmerize.

Fuck.

Rising, she stretched and checked herself for damage. Nothing she could feel. But then again, if she'd been out for days rather than hours, she might have healed.

How long had she been asleep? Last thing she remembered was getting caught like the dumbest of idiots, led into a trap. She'd known it was too easy, and yet she let herself be fooled.

She paced the glass cube holding her prisoner, unable to get a good stomp in due to the spongy floor. The cubicle held nothing, not a blanket or even a toilet. She hoped she didn't have to go.

Banging on the glass didn't vibrate the panels. Shouting sounded muffled.

Damn her for being an idiot. She should have at least sent Raymond a message. How long would he wait before realizing she wasn't coming back? Would he hide Sunshine? Or would he come looking for her? She wanted him to try, even as she knew it was foolish and selfish.

No one would be coming to her rescue.

The opaque glass suddenly cleared as if a switch had been thrown. Overhead, UV light shone and caused her to squint. Her skin tingled uncomfortably. It took a second to adjust her vision and notice the machines placed outside the cube. So many of them, and familiar too. Just like the lab she grew up in.

No one appeared, but she'd wager on there being surveillance. A glance overhead showed cameras suspended in all directions, watching her every move.

Knowing he spied didn't stop her from being startled when Mr. X said, "So nice to see you again, VX31."

The reminder of her previous identity—nothing

but a model number—made her flinch. In retaliation she replied with a double middle-finger salute.

"Is that any way to act given the trouble you've caused? You destroyed decades of research when you went after my labs."

She snorted. "Boo fucking hoo. I wish I'd done more sooner."

"It doesn't matter, you know. All you did was erase my failures and then were kind enough to return to me that I might continue my work."

"I won't help you."

"You already have. You had a child. Where is she?" The casual tone speaking as to the true reason for her capture.

"Don't know what you're talking about."

"Subterfuge is pointless when I'm aware of the child."

"So what if I did? It has nothing to do with you. Her dad is human."

"Lying won't help you," Mr. X stated. "She was conceived in the lab. My lab. Making her mine. You will give her back."

"You aren't getting anywhere near her." She'd suffer any torment to keep Sunshine safe. She had to believe that Raymond would know how to hide and protect her. It made Sunshine's calling him Daddy make sense. Her daughter must have known she'd lose her mother and would acquire a new parent.

It chilled Lainey to realize she wouldn't be around to see her daughter grow up. To explore the strange passion between her and Raymond. Perhaps he'd find someone new to form a family unit with Sunshine. Perhaps, with Lainey gone, they'd have a chance for a future.

"Grr." The rumble emerged from her as she paced her glass prison, and Mr. X mistook the cause.

"You do realize this process doesn't have to be painful. You should recall from before that if you cooperate with me, I can ensure you and the child both live comfortably." Mr. X sounded reasonable, and yet she wasn't gullible enough to believe his lies.

"You'd have us live as prisoners," she spat.

"Dangerous animals need a cage."

"We're not animals."

"The dead bodies you left behind say otherwise."

"Self-defense."

"And let's not forget hunger. Does the child need blood as much as you do? More? You left before we knew you were pregnant. Imagine my surprise when we realized you lived and discovered your secret. Excellent job of hiding her existence by the way. You might have gotten away with it but for one mistake."

"What?" She expected him to say Raymond. Even blame her destructive vengeance on the Xlabs as the thing that led Mr. X back to her.

But it turned out she was the one at fault.

"Before wiping the server at your original facility, you spent time snooping through your records, most specifically, the last in vitro attempt. Such curiosity about the father and I asked myself why unless the fetus lived. A woman and a child, hiding from the world. That narrowed things quite a bit."

Her stomach sank. "Leave us alone."

"I can't do that, and I think you know the reason why."

Her stomach twisted suddenly. She wanted to stop talking to Mr. X. Wanted to shut her ears before he divulged his sick plan. "You want to use Sunshine for your perverted experiments."

"On the contrary." Mr. X's voice lowered. "I want nothing more than to claim my firstborn daughter."

25

For a moment, Lainey couldn't say a thing. Then it emerged in a scream, "Liar!" It had to be a lie. Her stomach churned, and her throat tightened.

"Am I lying? Look at me, VX31. Look at me and see the truth."

Mr. X, wearing his metal face shield, entered the room through a door that hissed shut once he stepped inside. She moved to the glass wall and placed her palms against it.

He was so close.

So far.

Wearing a suit and his habitual mask. Did he even have a face?

"Show yourself, coward!" She slapped the glass.

"If you insist." He removed it without argument and without touching any straps.

Mr. X was the everything man. His features nondescript, the kind to get lost in a crowd. Until you looked into his eyes. No wonder he kept them hidden behind glasses. Anyone looking into them could see he wasn't entirely human. The red ring around the iris almost glowed and, when the white turned black, looking away became impossible.

A vampire, but of a more intense version than the hybrids she'd met. Much more powerful than herself.

He smiled at her shocked expression. "Surprised? Not what you expected I'm sure."

"You're a vampire!"

"Indeed, and practically the last of my kind. The last true vampire I came across ended up providing your gene markers."

"You experimented using your own kind?" she squeaked.

"Their deaths were for a noble purpose. And don't complain; they are the reason you exist."

"You made me a monster."

"Only according to humanity. Vampires are a species like any other."

"With a penchant for blood."

"And? Everyone has to eat." He tucked his hand behind his back and did a slow saunter in front of her glass cage. "Did you know that actual vampires were almost eradicated in the sixteenth century?"

"Boohoo. You almost got wiped out. Guess you'll have to rebuild your army of darkness."

"If only it were as easy as the movies claim. Vampirism isn't a virus but genetics."

"Vampires are born?" The very idea blew her mind.

"All living creatures are born so long as two compatible beings can mate. Going back to the great genocide of my kind, it led to a difficulty reproducing. The few stragglers I've encountered since that purge were all male. Which was biologically impossible for me to reproduce with. Lucky for me, science evolved, as did genetic splicing, providing me with the means to recreate a feminine option."

She almost gagged as she realized what he implied. "Me."

"You are but a pale end goal. A half-breed," he said with a sneer. "But my daughter, she is close enough to give me hope."

She tried to wrap her mind around the fact the Xlabs were about making female vampires to have babies. "If you wanted to make vampires, why create the shifters?"

"Because investors preferred the idea of creating super soldiers, especially once some of the issues with our vampire mixes emerged." His lip curled.

"Apparently, the ability to reproduce was stronger than their desire to live forever."

"I'd say the insanity played a part." Because as far as Lainey knew, she was the only vampire hybrid to remain sane past the age of twenty.

He waved a hand. "A hormonal imbalance that can be managed. And now that I can prove reproduction is viable..." He grinned. Pleasant and not showing the evil it hid.

"I'd hardly call one live birth a success. How many failed before that?"

"Is that a challenge to see if we can do it again?" His smile was too pleasant to be evil, and yet she felt a chill. "Just think, in a half-dozen years or so, the child will be of age to breed as well."

The very idea horrified. "She's your daughter."

"She is the answer to rectifying the wrong done to my kind. Of bringing back vampires that we might rule as we were meant to do."

Lainey had plenty to say about his disgusting plan; however a sudden beeping, strident and nonstop, tightened Mr. X's bland mouth. He brought his phone to his ear and barked, "What?"

His expression changed. His brows rose. And then he laughed.

"What's so funny?" she asked as he hung up.

"It would seem your lover has shown up and demanded entrance."

Her heart stopped in shock—and pleasure. Outwardly she said and showed nothing.

Mr. X didn't seem to notice. "How did you hook up with one of the Hubbards? Alaska and Ottawa aren't exactly neighbors. Doesn't really matter. I wondered who the man was I found you with. Guess we'll blame the storm for me not recognizing subject LN03. I'll bet he knows where to find the child."

Lainey slapped the glass wall and screamed, "Leave her alone."

"Or what?" Mr. X mocked. "Count yourself lucky you've proven useful. Or more accurately, your womb has. It's the only reason you're alive. And you'd better hope my daughter doesn't turn out to be a disappointment." He stepped out of the room.

Before Lainey could reply, the glass turned opaque and soundless. Meaning there was no one to hear her frustrated scream and then her gut-wrenching sobs.

26

PRETEND TO BE SOMEONE ELSE.

There was no other choice, even as there was much arguing about it. In the end, everyone agreed. It should be Raymond who knocked on the door at the address they'd found.

He went alone, wearing a parka and tuque along with air of excitement. There was something quite exhilarating about driving to the gates of a known enemy and demanding entry.

His heart raced a little faster than usual. His hands trembled, so he held on to the steering wheel tight enough to hide it.

He couldn't fuck up. Not now. He had too much to lose.

There was an intercom by the closed gate. "State your business."

"Tell Mr. X that Raymond Hubbard is here to see him."

"You have the wrong address," lied the voice on the other end.

"He wants to see me. Tell him it's LN03."

"Hold on." It took more than a minute before the security manning the intercom system returned and said, "Head for the house."

The mechanical gate opened, and he drove into the belly of the beast. Also known as Mr. X, his creator. The fucker who'd made them all because he thought he was some kind of god.

And now he was about to get taken out by his creations.

Getting here had proved a challenge. The phone stolen from the enemy had been impossible to crack. It was Sunshine who helped the most by unlocking Lainey's laptop.

No one had thought to ask her for a passcode.

Once they got in, they found the GPS address Lainey had mapped and researched. Knew where to go, the problem being, go in quietly or cocky?

The Hubbards weren't about to hide as everyone kept telling them to do. Nor would they let Mr. X continue to pose a threat. One only had to recollect Mom, wringing her hands, saying, *"We have to protect the babies."*

Only one way to do that.

Still, as he parked the rental and went up the wide stone steps, he rethought the plan to come in the front door. Who knew how many guns were trained on him? What if they shot him before he had a chance to do anything? He couldn't die now. Not when he'd found love. And what of the child?

A woman dressed in crisp gray—slacks, blouse, and even the shoes—answered the door before he could even knock and led him into a great room. It was two stories with windows overlooking a breathtaking vista: a green rolling yard with a creek bisecting it and sloping down to a wooded area.

He remained staring out the window even as he sensed someone entering the room. The hair on his nape prickled.

"If it isn't one of the Hubbards. So kind to put yourself into my hands. You've saved me the time and effort given I had higher priorities than your family."

"You mean like imprisoning people and threatening children?" He'd not forgotten the scare from when his little brother was taken.

"I wouldn't have to threaten if you'd do as you're told."

At that, Raymond chuckled. "You must have us mistaken with cowards. Haven't you realized yet? My family isn't afraid of you."

"You should be."

Outside the window, he saw movement at the edge of the forest. A wolf's muzzle followed by a sleek body.

No alarm sounded, but that didn't mean shit.

"Turn around," Mr. X ordered.

"Aren't those the lyrics to a song?" He procrastinated a little longer.

"Turn. Around."

The force in the command made him pivot. For the first time he beheld Mr. X, wearing a mask over his features. A man of average size and build.

The strange fellow muttered, "You're not Raymond."

"Nope," popped Dominick. "I'm his big brother, here to say leave Raymond the fuck alone."

With that, the former military man—who hadn't been frisked because apparently, his nerdy brother wasn't worth the trouble—withdrew his gun and blew a hole in the fucker.

What he didn't expect was for Mr. X to run away.

Uh-oh.

27

*R*AYMOND'S *L*IST OF *R*EASONS *T*O *S*TAY *H*OME, *#99: Netflix has all the thrills and chills a man needs.*

Raymond really needed a better coat. As he crept through the woods alongside wolves and his brother the tiger, he shivered inside his lumber jacket, chilled to the bone even with the layered sweater underneath. He took exception with how the movies made the heroes appear to infiltrate effortlessly, oozing confidence.

In reality, he was sweating. His stomach formed a knot that might never unwind, and he had a scream ready to launch if anything startled him.

He wasn't a hero, and yet, he had to become one. For Lainey.

She needed him.

Sunshine needed him to save her mom.

His family needed him to end Mr. X's reign of terror.

And he needed to do this to prove to himself he could be the man everyone needed. A man who could protect his family. With a bit of help.

The wolves spread out, ready to cover each corner of the house. Thus far they'd only encountered two patrolling guards. Trussed up and alive, but only if found before they froze to death.

While everyone chose a door and window, he had a strange thought that led him to the overly large cabana at the edge of the yard. Why one that big? A riding mower and a few tools for yardwork didn't require a building that was more than ten feet square with a chimney. He also spotted electrical wires rising from the ground and snaking inside.

For a shed.

With no windows.

Suspicions aside, he was drawn to it and he wasn't about to ignore the pull. The door was locked, no surprise. He hesitated only for a moment before placing the clay that Sunshine assured him would go kaboom around the knob and lock. Never mind how or why a child knew anything about explosives.

It uttered a large pop when it blew, and the door swung open.

Someone ran out with a gun. Raymond prepared

to get shot when a furry body soared from the side and tackled the man.

One down.

Raymond stepped inside, not surprised at the sight of the elevator that could only go down. Everyone knew secret labs doing nefarious things were kept in basements. A wolf joined him in that cab and did little to alleviate his disquiet. The first floor held a surprised guard, who opened his mouth to yell before Mr.—or was it Mrs.?— Wolf handled him.

Raymond found two empty labs and a room of vacant cages. Before he could go down another level, an alarm sounded and he heard the clanging of doors sealing shut and the elevator locked in place.

Once more, movies didn't fail him. He found the elevator hatch in the ceiling just out of reach.

The wolf shifted into a big, grimacing dude. "I'll give you a boost." He knelt and laced his fingers.

The hatch popped open, and Raymond grabbed the lip to haul himself through. He climbed down a level and pried open the doors. He knew he'd found the right place.

Four guards, armed and waiting, faced them.

The naked man showed no fear as he ran for them, changing into a wolf mid stride. The guards fired their weapons. Pain seared across Raymond's ear as a bullet skimmed part of it.

Then there was screaming. Not by him he was glad to say, but the guy getting bitten.

Another gun went off, and the wolf yelped, which jolted Raymond into action. He yelled as he rushed the guards, certain he'd get killed, only suddenly he was snarling and growling.

Then he was biting.

Lainey and Sunshine were right. It did feel good.

28

LAINEY THOUGHT SHE HEARD A MUFFLED gunshot. Maybe a scream. Then nothing until—

Bang. Something slammed the glass cube.

Thump. It cracked.

Smash. The prison opened, and there was Raymond, naked and wielding a fire extinguisher, a wild light in his eyes.

"Lainey!" he exclaimed, obviously happy to see her.

She burst into tears and couldn't have said why. Relief yes, but also something else she couldn't define. He'd come for her. Someone cared enough to rescue her, and it broke through every single wall she had.

She hugged Raymond until someone cleared their throat and said, "Um, we should probably leave."

Leaving sounded like a great idea.

Even as it turned out to be a little difficult. The lockdown meant they had to climb the elevator shaft with an embarrassed and naked Raymond insisting she go first.

At the top, the sealed doors wouldn't budge. They went back down a level and hunted around until they found not just some clothes but her purse —and its explosives.

They emerged into the yard, and a man yelled, "Raymond, have you seen him?"

"Seen who?" hollered Raymond. Then in an aside to Lainey, "That's my brother Dominick." Part of the rescue team Raymond told her about when he'd caught her up on their way out.

"Have you seen Mr. X?" Dominick asked, heading for them.

"I thought the plan was you kill him while I rescued Lainey," Raymond exclaimed with a fling of his hands.

"I shot him. Hole through the chest big enough to see daylight. He should be dead, but the fucker ran off, and now I can't find him."

Lainey wanted to sigh. "Full vampires are hard to kill."

"Vampire?" He had a dubious note to his query.

"Yes. And he's strong, too, for his kind. We'll have to take his head to make sure he stays dead."

"Is that the only way to kill him?" Raymond cast her a startled glance.

She shrugged. "Kind of hard to walk away with no brains to call the shots. I'd also recommend burning the body to be sure."

"A real fucking vampire." Dominick whistled. "I'll be damned."

"We all will be if we don't find him," was Lainey's grim response.

They spent the next few hours looking. The trail of blood from the house stopped suddenly in the snow, as if Mr. X had disappeared into thin air.

Eventually they had to call it off with Dominick and his werewolf crew agreeing to stay behind to search the house and lab some more before destroying it. Raymond was taking Lainey back to the hotel where Sunshine put together puzzles and drew pictures with her new grandma under the watchful eye of the werewolf on guard duty. Lainey had spoken to her kid less than an hour ago. She was safe. No one knew where Sunshine was.

Still, Lainey couldn't help her unease as they neared the hotel. "Call your mom," she said to Raymond.

"It's almost six a.m."

"They might still be up."

He called, and the line went to voicemail right away. "Hold on, I'll call again."

No reply.

Raymond drove faster, and Lainey said nothing as she tensed in her seat. At the hotel, she practically ran from the car and bounced in place, waiting for the elevator, which took its sweet time.

Raymond remained by her side, his anxiety as palpable as her own. She wasn't surprised to find the door to the room open. She cried out as he saw someone on the floor.

It took only a second to realize it wasn't Sunshine. An older woman lay prone, a gash on her head not as concerning as the holes in her neck, leaking sluggishly.

"Mom! Shit. Mom!" Raymond dropped to his knees beside her, drawing her into his arms, shaking.

Lainey shook, too.

Where was Sunshine?

She emerged into the hall and glanced both ways. Motherly instinct drove her to the stairs, and she went up. The rooftop access was locked, but she slammed into the door anyhow, and it opened, spilling her onto the rooftop.

And there he was, Mr. X with Sunshine's hand held tightly in his grip.

"Mommy!" her daughter shrieked. "Help!"

Understandable given the man by her side had a hole in his chest. But he wasn't dead. Pissed, though, and an angry vampire was a dangerous thing. Mr. X was missing his mask, and so she could see his eyes were black and his fangs long and sharp.

"There you are. I told the brat you'd come for her. Maternal instinct ever does lead to stupid actions."

"You've lost. Hand her over."

"Doesn't seem that way to me. I have the child."

A child terrified as she glanced at the lightening sky. Dawn approached.

It made Lainey sick to her stomach to imagine what would happen if she couldn't resolve this quickly. "Don't hurt her. Please." Her voice broke, and she hated herself for pleading, but this was her baby. She'd crawl across glass for her.

"Seems only fair. Look at what you did to me." He thrust out his chest, the hole moist and yet already showing signs of healing.

Sunshine whimpered as the sun pinked the sky.

"No." She ran for Mr. X, but he stared at her. His voice inside her head said, "Stop."

She froze mid-step, tears tracking down her cheeks as the dawn brightened.

Sunshine, trying to look brave, sounded terrified. "It's okay, Mommy."

How could it be okay? The UV light hit her daughter's skin, and it turned pink, then red. Mr. X was oblivious and uncaring as he slid his metal mask on then some gloves. "You made a grave mistake in thinking me benevolent. I grew up in a time of an eye for an eye. Although, in my case, my mantra is hurt me, and I'll kill you or someone you love."

"You need her. She's your daughter." Lainey didn't want to blurt it out, but she had to do something as Sunshine began to wail.

"I'll make another. One not corrupted by a mother's soft influence." Distaste colored his statement. "If it can be done once, it can be done twice," he boomed to make himself heard over the screams.

Sunshine's skin bubbled, and Lainey could only sob as her daughter writhed in the sunlight.

Mr. X ignored her to approach Lainey. "I won't make the same mistake twice. This time, you'll be strapped to a bed."

"Mommy!"

The final strident scream broke Lainey, and she sobbed, the vampire's compulsion shattering as grief took over. She hit the ground on her hands and knees, sobbing, her anguish stronger than her hatred. She wanted to die. Wanted him to die.

He needed to die. Before she could even try, she heard a strange noise, almost like a high-pitched clicking. It drew not only Lainey's attention but Mr. X's, too. He whirled around and breathed, "What the hell?"

"I think you mean, what the bat?" huffed Lainey in surprise, because Sunshine wasn't a little girl anymore.

As Mr. X approached the screeching creature, flapping its wings, Lainey pushed to her feet in time to see a rush of movement. Raymond sprinting past, a blade in hand, too fast even for Mr. X to react.

By the time that bastard whirled, his head went flying. It hit the ground and rolled. The body dropped to the rooftop. Raymond's knife-wielding arm lowered, and a squeaky voice yelled, "Mommy."

And for the second time in twenty-four hours, Lainey burst into tears.

Of joy.

EPILOGUE

~~RAYMOND'S LIST OF REASONS TO STAY HOME~~. *HOME IS with my girls wherever that might be in the world.*

Raymond and Lainey went to visit their new nieces at the hospital. He could have groaned to see Dominick acting as if he'd done all the work. The guy strutted and handed out cigars despite the fact none of them smoked, except for Nimway. She puffed outside and declared it some good shit.

Raymond took stock of the joy on his brother's face, the way Lainey's expression softened seeing the babies, thought of how much he loved Sunshine, his daughter. He finally understood why people had families. Because they made life worth living.

And Raymond wanted to feel alive. But only if he could have Lainey and Sunshine with him. The kid ran out of his mom's house when they arrived, waving a piece of paper.

"I drew a picture!" she said, her speech having grown leaps and bounds now that she was socializing more. No school, not with her allergy to sun, but the fall was when the days got shorter, and they'd already enrolled her in programs with other kids. He and Lainey had decided Sunshine deserved some stability and were in the process of house hunting for something more suburban than the farm.

Lainey gasped as she glanced at the drawing. "Ray!"

He understood her shock as he took in the details of the picture. It showed a little girl with silver-blonde hair gripping the rounded hands of a figure labelled Mom and the other, Dad. A moon hung in the sky over a house that looked an awful lot like the one a street over from his mom's, down to the red front door and the oak tree. Plus, one more detail: a stick baby in the mother's arms.

Named—

"Quasimodo?" Lainey inquired.

"Yes!" Sunshine clapped her hands. "My brother is Quasimodo. Like the hunchback of Notre Dame."

Thankfully, this was one prediction that didn't come true. His name was Quinn. And he was perfect.

Just like his family.

"You're looking sappy again," his wife of two months said.

"Thinking of how much I love you guys."

It turned out even a genetically modified geek could have his happily ever after.

And maybe that picture Sunshine handed him a few weeks ago of a world on fire would never come to pass.

I HOPE you enjoyed the Growl and Prowl series with three very different and intense heroes. Will there be more? We do have more Hubbards, after all…

You tell me. Who's next?

For more information or books (including many HOT shifters) see EveLanglais.com